Ning's Igloo Romance

Ning's Igloo Romance

A Sequel to
Ningiyuk's Igloo World

By

ANNA ROKEBY-THOMAS

MOODY PRESS
CHICAGO

ISBN: 0-8024-5936-6

Printed in the United States of America

To my children

Emily Ann

David

Derwyn

Contents

1

Plans for Ning

The big ship had come and gone to the tiny Arctic settlement of Cambridge Bay, on a desolate, northern island. The people were both glad and sorry. They now had their year's supply of groceries and other needs. But the ship's going meant they were again in isolation and shut off from the outside world.

The Eskimo who had come to meet the ship traveled back to their hunting grounds. Some paddled canoes, in comparative comfort, around the rugged shoreline. But many walked overland in groups, carrying heavy packs on their backs.

In one of the groups was Ningiyuk. She trudged along bravely beside her father and brother. "Everything is different now. The change has come like magic!" she exclaimed, breaking the silence.

Komoyiok looked up in surprise. "I see no change, Ning. Unless you mean the cold nip in the air at night-time. It always happens suddenly. A good thing for the huskies. They are bearing up much better with their heavy packs."

"It's the sun I'm talking about!" Ning pointed excitedly to the great, red ball that was sinking into the northern horizon. "On our way to the ship it was circling the sky. But now it is as tired as my sore feet. See! It's dropping into bed, behind the top of the earth, to have a sleep." Sadly she added, "I miss the sun more than anybody in the whole world. And each night it will sleep longer and longer."

"Who knows if it is sleeping or not?" Okio asked in his typical, older-brother way. "Why can't you just say that the midnight sun is done and over with for another year? It's a wonder you haven't stumbled and broken some bones, the way you keep watching the sun instead of where you are walking! One would think it belonged to you!"

"It does belong to me!" Ning was indignant. "And I feel great pity for the one in our family who speaks of the sun as though it were a common thing, like a—like a—a stone."

"Stop your quarreling." Komoyiok frowned. "It has been a long, hard trek, and you are tired. But we have only to climb yonder hill, and our tent settlement will be in sight."

Okio bounded ahead with his friends to see if it were true. But Ning stared at her father with amazement in her eyes. He knew everything! Did he see invisible signs to guide him over the rocky desert, where every stone and elevation looked so alike? Besides this, he could hunt and trap and fish better than any other man on the Arctic island. Tears welled up in Ning's dark eyes as her thoughts raced on. *And his heart is filled with love. For me! His worthless, adopted daughter.*

Then, almost as though a silent finger were beckoning, they both looked upward. But neither of them spoke, for

JNHOWARD

the spell of the sunset touching the dawn had come over them. Golden-pink rays burst into the sky. They sprayed silently to the west, bidding farewell to the sunset. Then, just as silently, they spread to the east and embraced the dawn. The sky grew pinker and pinker, and an invisible brush reached down and tinted their world.

The magic brush touched their cheeks, and a rosy glow turned the ugly rocks into sparkling jewels. Ningiyuk and her father stood there, staring at the beauty of it all.

Ning reached out and slipped her hand in Komoyiok's. "The Great Spirit is giving us a peek into the heavens," she whispered.

Komoyiok nodded in silent agreement. Then his thoughts came back to earth. "What a strange child you are." The strong man ruffled his daughter's hair and threw the heavy pack over his back.

"The tents! The tents!" Okio was shouting and waving. "We are almost home!"

"Yes, we are almost home," Komoyiok repeated. Hand in hand, he and his daughter walked until they reached the open flap of their tent door.

Ning fairly flew from her mother to her grandmother. She rubbed their noses with such a fierceness that it made them wonder if she had lost her senses on the trip. Then she insisted on pulling the sleeping baby from inside her mother's pouched *artigue*. "It *is* Kiyuk!" she squealed, as though it were a surprise. "He's as fat as a seal—and so big!"

"Come on! Let's make the rounds of the tents," Okio said, motioning to his sister. "Everybody is drinking tea and telling stories. If we add our tale about meeting the ship, it could become a legend!"

The moment the children left, Atuk handed her tired

husband new fur slippers to put on his weary feet. "What a load you carried," she scolded as she gave him a mug of tea. "But our children carried a bundle that *ookpik,* the owl, could have held in his claws."

"They are growing children and did well enough," he told her. Then, as he ate his tasty meal of dried fish and bannock, his thoughts drifted far beyond the tent. Neither the howling of the huskies outside nor the heavy snoring of his old mother at the far end of the tent disturbed his thoughts.

Atuk asked no questions. Indeed, a poor Eskimo wife she would be if she had. But she watched him closely out of the corner of her eye, and she waited for him to speak.

"Ningiyuk learned about her own father at shiptime," Komoyiok said, breaking the silence. Then he unfolded the whole story to his wife. "He has become rich and is now able to care for Ningiyuk. He wanted her to go and live with him in the west, and he offered me many foxes if I would let her go. But I wanted Ning to make the choice. She prayed to the Great Spirit, and He helped her to know that her place is here with us." With deep emotion he asked, "Is it not a great relief to you that she chose to come back to our igloo?"

"It is the choice I knew she would make." Atuk's strong face had turned pale, but she kept her feelings deeply hidden.

"I wasn't wise enough to know that she would come back to this lonely island of stone and blizzards." Komoyiok spoke gruffly. "Don't you realize she could have had the easy life of the west, right to her last, silly dream?"

"It wasn't this island that brought her back," Atuk stated, as a matter of fact. "We are her family. She is our child."

"Your words are well spoken," Komoyiok admitted. But he looked with some irritation at this wife of his. She kept so silent; yet she had a hidden source of wisdom that baffled him. Her masklike face seldom betrayed her feeling. It would be admitting weakness to tell her of the suffering he had gone through at the thought of losing Ningiyuk. Besides, it would be beyond her understanding.

Almost in answer to his thoughts, Atuk spoke out. "It is good that we will never have to give the child up. And now that we are really her parents, no time should be lost in choosing her a husband. You are her father." She looked straight into her husband's eyes.

Komoyiok jumped to his feet. "You have spoken out of turn!" His voice was trembling. "Ning is a child—scarcely more than a baby! I came back filled with happiness, but you would give that happiness away!"

A half-smile flitted across Atuk's serious face. "When springtime comes, Ning will have seen the sun return twelve times. And many of her friends will be married within the year."

"That's different. Those girls were promised in marriage on the day they were born. I need no son-in-law to help with the hunting. And I don't believe in child marriages." Komoyiok was pacing back and forth in the tent. Facing a bear could not have shaken him as those few words his wife had spoken. He stopped in front of her. "Speak out, woman. There is more on your mind. I must hear what you have to say."

Atuk dropped the caribou skin she had been scraping. She was trembling. "I am afraid for Ning. She is such a beautiful child, and almost a woman."

"That is to our credit," Komoyiok sighed with relief. "We have fed her well, and she bears no marks of hunger."

"You don't understand." Atuk was wringing her hands. "Many boys are looking at her with love in their eyes. Natsook, from the far east, couldn't hide his feelings from me, either at Christmas or Easter. And when Eotuk came up from the mainland, he lingered long after his caribou skins were traded, to look at her pretty face."

"Make yourself clear." Komoyiok demanded. "You have just told me that I should choose a husband for the girl. Both the boys you speak of are sons of good hunters."

"That is what I expected you to say, and it sends cold chills down my back." Atuk went on to explain, "Since Ning was two days old, she has seldom been out of my sight. When you took her on the trip to meet the ship, there was such emptiness in the tent, that the days seemed like years. I'm ashamed of my weakness," Atuk continued, covering her face with her hands, "but I keep having horrid dreams. In all of them you are giving her away to a man in a distant place. You are doing it because he is a good hunter and will bring honor to our family."

Komoyiok was speechless. Never had he seen his woman cry, so he turned his head to save her embarrassment.

Atuk could not control her sobbing. "I know she will marry. But if you would only arrange a marriage close to home! Your nephew is a fine young lad. I'm ashamed of my weakness, but my dreams frighten me so. How can I bear it when some good hunter takes her to far away places?"

Komoyiok knelt down in front of his wife. All the wrinkles and stress had vanished from his face. "Forget about your bad dreams. Never will I bargain my daughter off, even to a good hunter. And no young lover would dare to take her from our igloo!" Rubbing his brow,

Komoyiok remembered something. "The missionary teaches us that a girl should have some choice in picking her own husband. Have we not good reason to believe our child chooses well?"

"Koanna! Koanna! Thank you!" Atuk's tears vanished and she picked up the caribou skin.

"Let there be no talk of husbands in front of our girl. We want her in our igloo for a long time. I find much amusement in her silly chatter." Half under his breath, Komoyiok added, "But it's not as foolish as it sounds—not by any means."

Atuk nodded approval. She scraped furiously on the hide.

2

On Thin Ice

Once the excitement of homecoming was over, the weary travelers crawled into their sleeping bags and fell into a deep sleep. Before they opened their eyes, the sun had dropped again below the northern horizon and was making an eastward circle.

"I feel like a brand new person!" Ning sprang out of her fur bed on the tent floor. She shook her brother vigorously, "How can you sleep so soundly when there is work to be done?"

Atuk joined in. "Indeed, yes. Your father has gone to the lake to set nets for char." She handed him tea. "You should be with him."

"I'll go now." Okio gulped his tea and was dressed in minutes. He reached for some dried fish and hurried away.

"Now, don't laugh at me," Ning said, warning her elders of a surprise, "but a new feeling has come over me. I want work—I mean real, serious work!"

"And what do you call serious work?" Atuk looked very amused.

"I want to sew a fur outfit for my baby brother." Ning closed her eyes and gave them the picture she was seeing. "I can see Kiyuk as plain as day. He's dressed in white furs made by my own hands. The trousers are white rabbit skins, and the artigue is from soft, white fox pelts. A fox tail swings down the back of the parka. This makes him a little, white hunter. Can't you just see him a year from now?" she opened her eyes and asked excitedly.

Atuk's head went down to hide her smile. But Grandmother Itow's dull ears had heard every word, and she aroused herself. "It is music to my ears to learn that you want to sew. But what nonsense you speak! A rabbit's skin is for wiping one's face and hands. And you'll soon learn that fox pelts are best traded at the white man's store. These fancy furs you dream about will never wear well."

"My dreams are crashed!" Ning looked sadly at her baby brother lying naked on the fur bed beside her. "And the desire to sew might leave me. My fingers wouldn't work nearly so well on tough, old, brown hides."

Itow was pulling a roll of skins from beneath her sleeping bag.

"Keep your dreams about a white outfit, and about sewing."

When the skins were unrolled Ning gasped with delight. They were as white and beautiful as freshly fallen snow! And almost as soft as an Arctic bunny. "Where did you get them?" she asked.

"They are the underbelly of the caribou. Often I have said that each caribou hides this little patch of white for the babies of the Iniut, the People." Itow looked at them with great pride. "There is enough here for the outfit you dream about."

"You'll help me—please?"

A bright spark of interest came into the old lady's dull eyes. She handed Ning a small *ooloo* and taught her the proper way to hold it as she scraped bits of fat from the small pieces of hide. They needed lots of scraping to make them soft and pliable.

All the while Ning worked, she chattered about their trip and the excitement of shiptime. But never once did she mention that the choice of another world had been given to her. Already it seemed far in the past and her young head was filled with happy plans for the future.

"The summer is gone," Itow moaned a week later, when she awakened from her sleep. "The winters come earlier and get colder each year." She sat up in a huddle and rubbed her hands.

At the same time, Okio came dashing over the hill and announced that there was ice on the small lake. This news sent the children scurrying, like so many lemmings, to see if it were true. It was true! And their feet began to tingle in anticipation of sliding across the glassy surface on their seal-soled boots.

"It's next thing to being a bird!" Ning loved the ice, and she could almost see Kiyuk, dressed in his white fur suit, by her side. "Next year I'll pull him on a caribou skin and swish him around the ice. He'll look like a little white bunny, blown in the wind."

"But today you will all stay on solid ground. And until the ice is safe." Siksik spoke loud and gruffly for all to hear. He was an old and feeble man, but he knew the secrets of the ice as no one else. He would give the signal when the time came.

The children were back to check the ice the next day and the next. But it was not until the fourth day that they found the sealskin rope stretched across the shallow end of the lake. It would be moved back each day as the ice thickened. But in the meantime they would play and slide only between the rope and the shore.

Ning joined hands with her friend Mituk, and together they circled the area in easy, swaying motions. It would seem that they were wearing skates, but never had they seen such things, except in pictures of the white man's magazine. As more children gathered on the ice it began swaying in a wavelike rhythm.

"It's rubber ice!" they laughed with glee. "But it's safe. We even saw Siksik cross the center of the lake."

"Don't get any wrong ideas," Okio warned the crowd. "Siksik has some special understanding of ice. The rest of us would drown!"

Just at that moment a tiny boy went flying across the ice in front of Ning. He was sitting on a caribou skin, and it spun dizzily across the safety line, heading for the center of the lake.

Ning pulled away from Mituk and bounded toward the child. He reached out his arms, and Ning sent him scooting back to safety on his caribou skin. Only when she saw him being grabbed from the ice did she realize what she had done—and her own precarious situation!

Before she could move, fears attacked her from every direction. The ice was so thin and rubbery that it was sinking under her weight. Then, *whi-ish, crackle!* The sound of cracking ice paralyzed her.

"Help! Help!" she gasped, scarcely above a whisper. The sound of her own voice added to her fright.

Above the voices of the terrified children on the shore she could hear Okio speaking to her. "You'll be all right. Father Komoyiok is coming. Get down on your knees—easy. Spread out your legs and arms slowly."

Ning obeyed mechanically. But when her face touched the ice floor she was terrified. The ice was *so* thin. And under the thin layer were many fish, all staring at her with wide eyes and open mouths. They seemed to be inviting her down! She closed her eyes tightly. But still those fish were trying to entice her downwards!

Then Ning remembered the Great Spirit. How could she have forgotten Him? "Hello, Great Spirit. I'm in great trouble. Help me get off this ice—please. Drowning among the fish would be awful, and I'm so scared. I feel better now. But stay with me. Please!"

Komoyiok's voice reached Ning from the shore, loud and clear. "Siksik will bring you off the ice. You must do exactly as he says." Once again he repeated the words, "Do exactly as Siksik says!"

Tears spilled out of Ning's eyes at the sound of her father's voice. Oh, how she longed for him to come and carry her safely off! But no thought except to obey him entered her mind.

Looking through her tears, Ning could see Siksik shuffling toward her. In his hand was a long, finely braided rope made from sealskin. He spoke quietly, but she could hear his words. "Have no fear, little girl. This rope I carry is magic! It was made to rescue people off the ice, and the magic came into it in the making."

Sudden, whiplike cracking echoed in their ears, and Ning stiffened with fear. "It's only an angry rumble." Siksik told her soothingly. "The ice has to talk!"

But Siksik's progress had stopped. He was testing the ice in front of him very cautiously with his fur-clad feet. "You were very wise to lie down, and I'm going to follow your example." And as he spoke she watched him sliding, face downward, onto the ice.

JNHOWARD

Ning watched his every move, and much to her amazement, he became as nimble as a snowbird. His body zigzagged back and forth, but gradually he was coming closer. "Once upon a time a fat woman got stranded on the ice, just as you are stranded. She was so big that all the igloo doors had to be cut larger to let her in."

"Did she drown?" Ning waited breathlessly for his answer.

"No. No. I brought her back to safety—with this magic rope, of course."

Ning breathed easier. "I'll do everything you say." Her eyes were begging.

"Hold onto this rope—tightly." He flipped it toward her and it lay easily within her reach. "Now, as I start wiggling backward, you wiggle forward. No! Not on your knees. Pretend that you are a seal, and sort of swim along."

"I'm trying," Ning whispered. And she soon found herself imitating the old man. But they they were moving so slowly, and the distance seemed so long!

"You're as light as a feather. Just try not to pay any attention to the ice rumbles. We're being scolded for being so far out, but this magic rope will do the trick. Keep thinking of that."

"You're so—so kind." The frightened girl began to sob. Never again would she think of him as a cross, old man with a leather face.

"Keep your tears for your sleeping bag. Surely you don't want your family to see you crying?"

"We've so far to go that my tears will be dried." Then Ning saw a funny grin come over her rescuer's face. He was on the safety zone, and with one, swift tug, he pulled her across. Shakily they got to their feet, for they could now walk to safety.

Ning's impulse was to run to her waiting father and cry on his shoulder. Instead, she held Siksik's bony hand and walked with him at a slow pace. As they went, she closed her eyes and talked with the Great Spirit. "Thank You for staying with me. And thank You for Siksik. Thank you—for everything!"

3

The Magic Rope

Komoyiok's skin tent was fairly bursting at the seams. There had almost been a tragedy, and all the settlement people tried to gather in. This was something that must be talked over.

"Koanna! Koanna!" Tuliak thanked Ning profusely. "I am the foolish one that sent Taktoo spinning across the ice. I couldn't believe my eyes when he went heading for the middle of the lake. And there you were, following close behind!"

"Next year I'll be playing with Kiyuk on the ice," Ning laughed shakily. "I guess that's what made me run so fast!"

"A pity you didn't run back as fast, instead of standing there with all your weight on one spot." Okio was ready with superior advice. "Instead, you caused all this commotion!"

"If it was that easy, you should have come out to rescue me!" Ning was in no mood to be teased. Besides, everybody was looking at her as though they expected her to be changed.

"You're a very brave girl!" Tuliak was on her side

and could not hide his admiration. Somehow, he had always thought of her as Okio's little sister. But from now on he would think of her differently, and he kept repeating his thanks.

Komoyiok was frowning, and his face was like a thundercloud. It did not please him that a fifteen-year-old boy was hanging around his daughter with such grateful eyes. "You young fellows can get over to the other tents and bring their kettles of boiling water," he almost barked at Tuliak. "The womenfolk are having a *mug-up* here."

"Where is Siksik?" Ning searched the crowd with her eyes. "I haven't thanked him properly." Even in the midst of all this excitement, she kept thinking about his magic rope. She wanted to examine it and have a talk with him.

"Let him be," Komoyiok told her. "I've been to see him in his tent. He has had his tea and wants to sleep for the rest of the day."

The gathering turned into a celebration. The people chewed on hardtack, and mugs of tea were sipped noisily. Stories were sure to be told, so one by one, the people sat down on their haunches. They were not disappointed, for every hair-raising escapade was plucked from the past and brought to light. The children had no idea that the ice held such power—and so many exciting stories!

When it seemed that there was not another story left to be told, Angulak asked if he might speak. This was very strange, for Angulak was old and shy. In the past he had always avoided telling stories. The people urged him to talk, and then waited in silence.

"When I was the age of this child who was rescued today, I, too, had an experience on ice." His mind drifted back. "It was springtime, and there was ice in the bay.

Like all children, my little brother and I played on it from morning until night with our husky pups. Even when water cut a channel in the bay we played on the ice floes attached to the shoreline. There were birds above, and the world seemed filled with sunshine and laughter.

"Then suddenly one day our happiness ended. An ice floe snapped between us, and as clearly as though it happened yesterday, I can see my brother's outstretched arms before he stepped into the angry waters. I stood there watching his frightened eyes go down—and we were separated. No comfort came to my heart when I was told the evil spirits had won a victory."

There was much mournful sympathy in the tent. "It is no wonder that you held such fears of the water spirits in your heart," one listener murmured.

"Do you still hold such fears?" Okio asked in deep wonder.

"Indeed, no. Since the stories of the man Jesus have come to our ears, we know that the evil spirits have no power to snatch us through the ice. They are not there! Now it seems strange to me that we ever held such bitterness and fears because of the spirits of the waters. Do we hate and fear the bitter winds and the blizzards and the polar bears? Indeed, we don't. Yet, they would snatch our lives in a second if we would but give them the chance. We arm ourselves to fight them with cunning and wisdom.

"We would do well to learn the dangers of the ice from Siksik, for it is part of our very lives. We play on it as children. We fish through it, and we entice the seals to emerge in the tunnels that they have kept open. And how else could we sled to the mainland to visit our southern tribes and trade for caribou skins, if it were not for the road of ice?

"Water, ice, bears, and blizzards! They are the heritage of our ancestors. Would they want us to be fearful or ashamed of these things?"

"No! No!" the people shouted. "You have taught us a great lesson." They shuffled back to their work in a thoughtful mood.

That night Ning found it hard to sleep. She rolled and tossed, and she had terrible dreams. Those eager fish were waiting and watching for the ice to break. She could feel herself falling down, down. Then the magic rope appeared! She touched it, and almost as though she were a feather, she floated back to safety.

Long after Ning was awake, she kept her eyes closed, for her mind was in the greatest turmoil, and she was trying to figure out the strange power of the magic rope. Only yesterday it had saved her life! Or had the power been in Siksik, who had manipulated the rope?

In her conflict the words of the missionary came ringing in her ears. Last year, because of a head injury, she had spent some weeks at the mission, and they had had many long talks. One day she had tried to convince the missionary there was real magic in the sun. "It's not only because my ancestors believe in magic, here and there. But I can *feel* the magic in the sun," she had told him. "And it's not sun worship!"

But the missionary had smiled and tried to explain, "The magic you speak of is the love of God. He made the sun, and all things are created by Him. Call it magic, if you must, but God does work in mysterious ways and He performs many wonders. You'll feel the magic of His works as you grow older, especially in times of trouble."

Ning sprang to her feet as more words came pouring into her mind. "I must talk with Siksik," she called back to her mother from the tent door, and her feet hardly touched the rocks as she sped across the settlement.

Inside the old man's small tent, Ning was shocked at what she saw. His wife, Arluk, was blind, and their few possessions were worn and meager.

"Have some tea." Siksik did not seem surprised at her entry. After he helped his wife to some dried fish, they all sat around the seal-oil lamp-stove.

"I came to thank you." Ning was quick to speak. Impulsively, she offered to do something in return. Siksik's tent looked so neglected and compared so poorly with her own, she wondered if she could help to improve it.

Siksik shook his head. "There is no need to thank me. I told you yesterday that the magic rope would do the trick."

"But I don't think your rope is magic," Ning said, trying not to be rude to the old man. "I think it's nothing more than a rope."

"You don't think my rope is magic! Everyone else does. And did it not save your life yesterday?"

"No!" Ning was definite. "It was the Great Spirit that saved my life; but He used your hands, and the rope."

"But the magic rope hauled you to safety. Now, didn't it?"

"Only because I hung onto it tightly," the child tried to explain. "But all the while I was talking with the Great Spirit. He guided you to use the rope wisely."

Siksik's face crinkled into a strange smile. "Then why didn't your father go out on the ice with a piece of rope? Would the Great Spirit not have guided him?" he asked.

Ning looked baffled. "I am very young, as you know, and am lacking in wisdom. But I asked the missionary many questions last summer." She hesitated and then went on to share her knowledge. "God is so full of love that He gives each of His children a talent. And although you are a grown man, you are still one of His children, since you have invited Jesus into your heart. Is it not a strange feeling to be a child and an old man at the same time?" Her dark, serious eyes looked into his.

"It's a good feeling," Siksik was quick to answer. "The message of the Great Spirit is so good that sometimes doubts enter my mind. When this happens the evil spirits seem to spring from the darkness, and I tremble with fear. But when I feel the weakness of a child, the strength of the Great Father comes to me. But what is this thing you call a talent?"

"It's a special gift that God gives us. I don't mean that it's a present of pelts or seal meat. It's a kind of power or instinct to do some part of God's work especially well. As you know, my father is a great hunter and can almost find the bear's den in the darkness. Some of our men have the knowledge to cure sick dogs, and others can smell a blizzard when it is still far off. Is this not so?"

Siksik nodded thoughtfully. He waited for her to say more.

"But you, Siksik, have a special understanding of the ice. It is such a mystery to our people that they like to believe the power is in your rope. That is why everyone calls it the magic rope!"

Ning knelt down in front of the old man. "But the magic is your gift from God. If you had not worked hard and studied the secrets of the ice, God would have taken the gift away from you. But all these years you have been using it to help other people." She laid her head on his knees and added, "I know the Great Spirit must be very

JNHOWARD

happy that you didn't waste His gift. And I can never thank you enough for using His gift to save my life."

Siksik placed his knobby, work-worn hands on her head. His eyes were misty. "Never have I heard such words from a young one. They have touched the heart of an old man."

4

Ning Adopts a Grandfather

Before leaving the tent, Ning went over to Siksik's wife and embraced her with pity and affection. Arluk had been sitting as still as a soapstone carving, staring through her sightless eyes. Her ears were dull, and she lived in a world of loneliness. She patted the child, and then her gnarled hands clung to Ning's as though she were afraid to let them go.

The couple's sad plight melted Ning's tender heart, and a desire to do something tangible came over her. How could she use her talent for their good? Was she not a mere Eskimo girl? Then words rushed into her mouth, and she spoke impulsively. But first she held Sisksik's hand as though she were taking a solemn oath. "I would like to be your granddaughter! Will you be my adopted grandfather?"

Siksik was silent. He could hardly believe his ears. "A poor grandfather I'd make," he said at last. "I'd be like a cross bear every time you stepped out of line."

"Then you will be my grandfather!" Ning threw her arms out with joy. "Now I can play on the ice as much as I like. My new grandfather will come running with his magic rope!"

"Be careful, little girl. The next time I come running with the magic rope it will be to lay it over your backside!" And Siksik laughed as he had not laughed in years.

Ning was hardly inside her own tent when she tried to tell the news, almost all in one breath. "Guess what? I've a grandfather now! Siksik has agreed to take me for a grandchild. Isn't that—"

She stopped short. Atuk was staring at her with an incredulous, shocked expression. *Whyever does she need to look like that, when all I did was adopt a grandfather?* Ning wondered. Her suspense did not last long.

"That poor man you want for a grandfather has no family, and he is old and frail. And did you not know his wife is both deaf and blind? I don't think you realize what you have done."

"But I thought—" Ning stammered.

Atuk waved her to silence and stood looking down at the tent floor for a long time. When she raised her head, her face looked brand-new, for she was wearing one of her rare smiles. "You did right, child. It's time that somebody adopted them, and I'm surprised that he would agree. All our women have been trying to help, but we've never known such independence. This just might be the answer."

Atuk knew well that it would be added work for herself, but the words of Jesus had come to her, "I was hungry but you didn't bring me food. My clothes were worn thin, but you didn't sew new ones" (Matthew 25:42-43). This new responsibility gave Atuk such a warm feeling that her cheeks glowed. She tightened the belt of her artigue so that Kiyuk would be secure, and headed for the ice to jig for fish.

Grandmother Itow sighed loudly from her corner in

the tent, and Ning went over and sat beside her. Ever since coming back from their trip, Ning had seen all too little of this woman she loved so well. Kiyuk was so amusing, and there seemed always to be excitement in the settlement. She laid her cheek against her grandmother's and gave her a bear hug. It was then she noticed how thin Itow was.

Ning sat back and looked her over from head to toe. At the same time prickly feelings of fear began running up and down her spine. The dearest grandmother in the whole world was fading away, like a flower at the end of summer. *Why has no one warned me?* she felt like crying out.

"You look weary, and there are lines of pain written on your face," Ning said gently. "Is it because your joints creak every time you move?"

"I feel the cold worse than a newborn baby," Itow said, rubbing her bluish hands, "and my aches and pains are because of my old age."

"The tent is cold and drafty since the cold weather has come. Soon there will be snow for igloos, and you're always happier in an igloo, aren't you?" Ning tried to convince herself that Itow was low in spirits and that an igloo would be the remedy. "You sit alone too much. I'm going to be better company for you from now on."

"It's company enough to see you come and go and to hear you sing." Itow patted the child's firm cheek. "But I have warnings that I will soon be in the happy hunting grounds."

"No! No!" Ning cried out. "You mustn't talk like that. We need you here with us."

"But it's a better place I go to." Itow smiled. Her thoughts were far, far away.

Ning sat with tears streaming down her cheeks, and her body shook with silent sobs. Down deep she knew that her grandmother's words were true and that before she was much older she would have to learn to live without a grandmother.

"Do you remember how you wept last year when the sun went away for the winter?" Itow reached out and touched the girl's hand. "One would think that you were parting with it forever, but you greeted it in the spring with joy, just as I said you would."

"I remember well. And you taught me a folklore song that will be written in my heart to the day I die." A happy thought flashed into Ning's mind. "I'll write a folklore song for you! It might take a long time, and it will be poor in comparison to yours. But it will be from my heart to yours."

"I'll be waiting for it. I started before I was your age to make up folklore, and glad I am that I did, for many messages have been passed on to our people." Itow's thoughts drifted back to the past, and she was lost in her world of dreams. Then she roused herself. "There is work to be done. If you stay by my side we might finish Kiyuk's white outfit before the day is finished. Then we must be scraping hides for an outfit for your new grandfather. He still goes out fishing and trapping in furs that are thin and tattered."

"And after that will you help me to make one for Arluk?" Ning's eyes were filled with stars. "We'll make hers especially pretty, even though she can't see, her fingers will feel the pattern and the softness of the fur."

Nothing pleased Itow more than to be helping and teaching this granddaughter of hers. "How you have changed from a year ago. For awhile I wondered if you

JNHOWARD

would ever draw stitches of sinew through a hide without pricking your fingers."

"I've had a good teacher!" Ning laughed. "Besides, I'm almost grown up now. Last year I was nothing more than a little girl."

"You'll always be a little girl to me—my little girl." Itow was thinking out loud.

It seemed to Ning that having a grandfather made the time fly by faster than it ever had before. Each day she went to Siksik's tent carrying a small pot of hot fish or caribou stew. But it was when she brought Atuk's famous *bannock* that old Arluk chuckled with delight. During each visit Ning kept a sharp lookout for the old couple's needs. And Siksik no longer scolded her for keeping their tent tidy.

Back in her own tent, Ning sewed beside her grandmother for a good part of each day. Never in her whole life had she felt so happy and content.

Finally, after much hard work and many bleeding fingers, Siksik's outfit was finished. The caribou fur was soft and thick, and there was even fancy trim around the bottom of the artigue. There was snow on the ground and Ning ran over the drifts to deliver her surprise. "It fits perfectly!" she squealed with delight when he had tried it on. "And to think my grandmother took your measurement out of the corner of her eye!"

At first Siksik was speechless; then he was embarrassed. When words came to him he said, "You spoke to me about the gift called a talent. Surely the Great Spirit will never take yours away. You have more than one; and they are growing, for you use them well."

But it was Arluk who was overcome with emotion. She hid her face in the soft warmth of the fur, and tears poured out of her blind eyes. When no more tears would come she examined the stitches and the trim with her fingers. "My man will be kept warm. My man will not feel the cold." It was the first time Ning had heard her speak since she had gone blind.

"You, too, will have a new outfit of furs before Christmas," Ning shouted in her ears. But the old lady shook her head and pulled at her fur sleeping bag. She was trying to say that it was all she would be needing.

That night Arluk died in her sleeping bag. Siksik walked slowly to Komoyiok's to tell the news, and like the wind it was soon all over the settlement. No one wept. But they put on their best furs and followed the sled that carried Arluk's body to the highest hill. Still in her sleeping bag, she was placed in a grave of stones. Komoyiok led them in prayer, and they sang their best loved hymn, "Jesus Loves Me."

One by one the people straggled back to the settlement, until Siksik stood alone with his thoughts at his wife's cold grave. Ning was waiting partway down the hill, and she ran back the moment she saw him move. She held his hand and led him to her father's tent.

"My tent will be lonely and bleak, and I don't have the courage to go back into it," he said bluntly.

"No one wants you to go back and live there alone," Komoyiok said, reaching out for his hand. "You belong here with us. Has our child not adopted you?"

"No. No." Siksik would not accept. "Your tent is full, and I can find contentment alone. But I have examined the snow drifts, and the blocks would shape into an igloo. That is the answer."

Komoyiok rubbed his brow. "It is time we all moved inland and set our traps for *tereguneak,* the fox." He clapped his hands to draw attention to the tea-drinking crowd. “Pull down your tents, and pack up. Tonight we will build an igloo village and sleep on snow platforms.”

5

Promoted in a Blizzard

Excitement was in the hearts of all the people, for to move on was their way of life. The fishing in the river had been good, and the seals had been plentiful. But now it was igloo time! The children ran hither and yon as they helped to pack all their worldly goods atop the big sled.

In the midst of it all Ning and Okio had a quarrel—not just one of their everyday arguments, but one that ended in Ning being shaken until her teeth clattered.

"I'll tell our father about this." Ning was trembling with rage. "And you'll answer for your temper!"

"You'd be the sorry one, for you'd get more than a shaking from him for what you've done."

Ning seemed confused. "All I did was feed Koko one little fish! You know it will be hard sledding today, and Koko is my favorite dog. And for many good reasons!"

"But you've been doing it all summer, even though I've warned you not to." Okio was grim and serious. "Can't you understand that Koko is now our lead dog and that someday our very lives may depend on her? Your foolish favors have made her fat and lazy and almost useless.

Huskies are to be fed once in the evening, and there should be no coddling or favoritism."

"You favor Karsuk! He snarls and snaps like a wolf, but your eyes are filled with pride every time you look at him."

A smile broke over Okio's face, for Ning was right. "Karsuk is still an overgrown pup, but he will settle down soon. I can see in him the makings of a lead dog—I mean a great leader. One that will blaze the trail with courage, through storms and blizzards, and fight his way into a bear's den without the whine of fear."

"I believe you're serious!" Ning was amazed to hear his words. "But in the meantime, keep in mind that Koko is lead dog. Your favorite overgrown pup is scarcely more than sled broken."

"Time will tell." Okio's face was grim again.

"I'm sorry," Ning said contritely, for the truth of Okio's lecture was sinking in, and it frightened her. I'll never overfeed Koko again. And don't tell Father Komoyiok-- please."

"We shouldn't quarrel, little sister." Okio was repentant for losing his temper. But their dog team was increasingly important to him, and he jealously guarded their fitness and health.

A few hours later eight sleds pulled away from the deserted settlement, and the men found the sledding better than they had anticipated. Before nightfall they were inland and had found what seemed like a good trapping area. The menfolk had a small conference and decided to make it their home until the Christmas exodus.

Once the decision was made Ning helped her old grandmother down from the highly loaded sled. Itow seemed almost in a daze and staggered to keep her balance. "I keep thinking of the happy hunting grounds when I look around me," she said.

"It's because of the pure whiteness," Ning whispered. There was something awesome about virgin snow as far as eye could see. They stood watching the sunset together, and Ning sang a little folklore song as the words came into her heart.

> The snow is white, and the sky is bright;
> The fox is white, and his tail is light;
> The bear is white, and he growls all night.
> The igloo is white; we'll sleep at night.
> Our world is white; it's pure, pure white!

"Koanna! Thanks!" Itow felt that this child was a part of herself, for she had sung almost those same words as a child.

"But it's not my *real* folklore song," Ning said, taking Itow's hand. "I'm working hard, but I keep wondering if I can ever make one that is worthy of you."

As the sun went down the igloos went up, and above, the moon appeared, casting a golden glow over the whiteness.

Inside the family Igloo, which was like a beautiful dome carved from snow blocks, the flame of the seal-oil stove was heating a pot of water. Hot tea brought new life to the travelers, and never had frozen fish tasted so sweet. On the elevated platform the caribou skins were spread, and the tired family crawled into their sleeping bags.

"It's too pretty to sleep!" Ning exclaimed. She was watching imaginary fairies chasing back and forth on the sparkling snow walls, as the spluttering light sent out friendly shadows. "A tent is a necessity for the summertime. But an igloo is our home!"

JNHOWARD

"Yes. Yes. An igloo is our home." Other voices echoed her words, and silence fell over them all.

When morning came everyone was very busy filling in the chinks of their new homes and preparing for the stormy blasts that were sure to come. Ning felt a restlessness and could not settle down to anything as unexciting as sewing skin. She visited Siksik in his cozy igloo and then began a round of visiting all the igloos. But between visits she was surprised to see Okio hitching their dogs to the family sled.

"Can I go with you, wherever you're going?" She asked.

"Indeed, you can't. Tuliak and I are on our way to set fox traps. It will be no joy ride." And he reminded her in his most older-brother tone that girls did not go trapping.

"Just this once—please! You know I've been working very hard this season. Let me ask Mituk, and then we'll really have fun." Ning was very persuasive.

Okio hesitated. "I don't think our father would be pleased." Then he remembered that his sister had gone with them on a sealing trip, and all had gone well. "Well, just this once. And only if you get permission."

Ning raced away to ask Atuk's permission and soon came back with Mituk at her side. What excitement to move into an igloo village and go trapping with the boys, all within a few days! The four of them piled onto the heavy sled, and Okio flourished the whip. They were off, singing songs and laughing as the sled went bumpety-bump over the drifts.

One after the other they set their traps and concealed them in a cavity in the snow. They were covered with a layer of whittled snow that was scarcely thicker than a pane of glass. Tempting bits of seal were sprinkled about, and hopes ran high that the cunning fox would be tricked.

When the last trap had been set, the young folks sat on the sled. They ate some fish that the girls had brought along and nibbled on snow to quench their thirst. In the midst of their laughter Tuliak sprang to his feet. Angry clouds were gathering for a storm, and snow was swirling across the wastes. At the same time, the dogs were giving warning signals, for the smell of a blizzard had reached their noses.

"We better get home—fast!" Tuliak warned.

"Hold tight," Okio was turning his team around, and with the crack of the whip he shouted, "Mush! Mush!"

Blasts of wind attacked them from every direction as the dogs bounded forward into the darkening storm. Soon the snow was blinding, and the dogs began to falter as though uncertain of their direction. Okio was urging them desperately, but their pace became slower and slower, until they came to a full stop.

"I'll go up front and encourage the leader," Tuliak suggested.

"You'll get lost if you leave the sled. We might all be lost!" Mituk cried out in panic. "I wish our fathers were here."

"My brother can handle the dogs like any man." Ning spoke loudly. "We have a fine team, so stop your crying."

"It's too early for a real blizzard." The boys put up a brave front. But there was not much to be encouraged about, for the dogs were balking, and the wind was fierce, and over all hung the darkness of night.

"I know my own dogs," Okio decided. "The rest of you stay right on the sled, and I'll go up front." Slowly he felt his way along the line of dogs, talking to them all the way as though they were people. But he was gripped with alarm when he reached their lead dog. There was Koko, all curled up like a fat, fur ball, with her nose tucked under her paws. Try as he would, Okio could not make her budge. *What does one do with a dog that fears the blizzard and is too lazy to lead her team?*

At that very moment Okio heard a sound that was music to his ears. It was Karsuk howling to get home. "That's my leader!" Okio stripped Koko's harness off and half-dragged her back to Karsuk's place. Without any preparation, and in the fury of a storm, Karsuk became lead dog.

"Home, boy! Home!" Okio was back on the sled.

Karsuk leaped forward with a giant spring. Each pair of dogs behind him were, in turn, jerked to their feet and without hesitation or protest were following their leader. The sled barely touched the snow drifts as they streaked through the darkness.

"We're flying!" Ning giggled hysterically. All four were hanging onto the sled for dear life, but fearful thoughts were racing through their minds. Did this wild, overgrown pup know where he was taking them? Should they get off and dig themselves into a drift?

Suddenly the sled came to a full stop, and they were almost thrown off. What had happened? A chorus of howling huskies reached their ears. It was the chorus of, "Welcome home!"

Ning and Mituk hugged each other and cried with joy.

"Three cheers for Karsuk!" Okio shouted above the wind.

6

Darkness Strikes

Ning felt so much like a hero that had reached safety in the nick of time, that she scurried through their snow tunnel to claim her welcome. But she was in for a shock. Father Komoyiok was pale with anger. "Traplines are no part of your life! Your place is home with your mother!" was her greeting.

"But the storm came up so suddenly," Ning tried to explain.

"It's not the storm I'm talking or thinking about. I will not have you traipsing around on sleds unless I am with you. We would have felt shame if the four of you had dug yourself into a drift for as long as the storm lasted. Do you understand what I expect of you?" he asked severely.

"I think I do." Ning hung her head, but actually she thought it very strange that he should be so cross.

"I should never have given her permission." Atuk spoke quietly. "This will never happen again."

For the rest of the day and into the evening Ning was both silent and contrite. But try as she would, the only guilt she could feel was the harm she had done to Koko.

Her brother's point about fat dogs becoming useless was all too true, and she shuddered to think of what the consequences might have been. "I simply hate myself!" she said under her breath. But the void in the igloo continued, for it seemed like an empty dome when Ning did not talk.

"It didn't work!" she laughed out loud suddenly and spontaneously. The whole family came to a sharp attention, and Okio went so far as to ask her if she had lost her senses.

"I was trying to hate myself. But I'm not all that bad, so there was no use in trying," she said. seriously.

"Why don't you let someone else be the judge?" Okio asked.

"It's just like you to speak out of turn. The reason I couldn't hate myself was because I kept thinking about you!" The silence was over, and she went into raptures as she once more held the attention of the family. She was looking mostly at her father. "You should have seen the way he handled those dogs! No one else would have dared to put their faith in a wild, growling pup. But Okio did! Just as Siksik holds secrets about the ice, the boy in our igloo understands his dogs. He—"

"You chatter too much." Okio was embarrassed.

"I can't stop with those meager words!" She had more to say. "With Okio driving the team I knew we would get home safely, in the end. But not Mituk. She kept whimpering for her father. Finally, I had to tell her who knew what about dogs and driving. Didn't I, Okio?"

"All I have to say is that Karsuk didn't hesitate. He knew the way and brought us back safely. It was an ill wind, but it found us a good leader. I can start training him, can't I?" Okio looked at his father.

Komoyiok nodded approval, but he was watching Ning

out of the corner of his eye and hoping that she would unfold more of the vivid tale. His anger was gone, for how could one stay angry with such a child? She had been foolish, of course, but here she was praising her brother from the bottom of her heart. He sighed with relief that not once had she mentioned Tuliak.

The family listened to the story of the storm.

"And there we were, clinging together on the sled, for we knew right well if we ever fell off, the darkness would swallow us, and we'd freeze into statues. It would have been instant death! But we had no idea if we were going east, west, north, or south. I had visions of ending up on the sea ice and never being heard of again. It was a terrible situation to be in! But Okio—"

"It wasn't all that bad," Okio interrupted. "You always make things sound worse than they are. What kind of a story would you have to tell if it had been a real blizzard?"

"The storm is blowing itself out now," Komoyiok said; he could tell by the sound of the wind. Ning's lively story would ring in his ears long after she was asleep, and he felt new pride toward his son. But he would be a poor father if he showed his feelings, so he spoke to them gruffly. "Get into your sleeping bags. There is much work to be done in the days ahead."

The days were busy and they grew shorter and shorter. The sun became a slanting arch in the southern sky, and it gave out such feeble rays that shadows failed to appear. This made the light both faint and deceiving. One day, when Ning was on her way to Siksik's igloo, she screamed with fright. *"Nanuk! Nanuk!* The bear!" Men came running with their guns, but the mirage that had seemed so real turned out to be a trembling lemming.

"Anyway, I'm not going to cry this year when the sun

is gone," she confided in Mituk, "for if it didn't leave, it wouldn't come back. Imagine living in a world where you couldn't greet the sun after the darkness."

"We're too old to cry about—things." Mituk had swollen eyes. "Last night I cried myself to sleep, but it didn't help anything."

"Why were you crying?" Ning knew that her friend did not love the sun as she did, so she could think of nothing else Mituk would cry about.

"I'm to marry Nigvik at Christmas. Our fathers arranged it long ago." Mituk sighed in resignation. "Since he lives on the mainland and I've only seen him a few times, I had almost forgotten. But my father reminded me last night."

"But you look so sad!" Ning felt squeamish, for Mituk was only two years older than herself. She felt chills going up and down her spine.

"I don't want to go so far away and live among a strange tribe. Besides, I'll miss you." But being Eskimo girls, they tried hard not to show their emotions.

"You'll like living among the caribou!" Ning knew it was a silly thing to say, but it was the first thing that came to her mind. "And I'll never stop coaxing my father until he takes me down to visit you." She could think of nothing else to cheer her friend, but she was going to think things over and have a long talk with her father.

But before two more weeks had passed, neither Mituk's sadness nor watching the sun slip off the world seemed of much importance. An unexpected enemy had come stealing upon their tribe with strange weapons, and it threatened their very lives. It was hunger.

One gale followed another, and swirling snow left mountainous drifts zigzagging crazily across the barren wastes. Not even the old men could remember a time of so many storms and so little food. They had lived through blizzards and hunger, but never had they gone on and on like this. Every time the men ventured out, they were driven back to the safety of their igloos.

Finally, when their food and heat were at a dangerously low ebb, the men decided to face staying out in the elements until a seal could be wrestled through sea ice or bears found in their dens. They would stay in groups of three, and at the risk of their lives they would fight the storms until they won an existence for their families.

Okio, Tuliak, and Etak, the three teenage boys, were left in charge of the settlement. They felt it an insult to their manhood and did it under protest.

"We'll sit here twiddling our thumbs while our fathers face the darkness and the dangers alone!" Okio spoke for the three of them.

"We'll have the women and children to keep us company." Tuliak tried to laugh, but it fell flat.

"Don't forget the old folks and the dogs," Etak added.

But nothing they could say would change the minds of the men. "It's our only comfort to know you are all three back here safe. Since you are still young, you have no idea of the responsibility that rests on your shoulders," Komoyiok tried to explain. "You will have to ration very carefully the bit of food that is left. When there is no longer food, you will kill the dogs, one by one, to keep life in everybody in your care."

Okio flinched at the thought of killing any one of their precious dogs. But Komoyiok pointed his finger at him. "You'll not be twiddling your fingers. It's the work of men we leave to be done."

The days dragged on and on as their hunger pains grew

JNHOWARD

stronger. Never had they felt such gnawing and twisting in their stomachs. The children no longer played but lay in their sleeping bags to conserve their strength. Atuk boiled the skeletons of foxes and any bones she could lay her hands on, but at best, there was little strength in the weak broth. And soon the flame from the seal-oil lamp became too feeble to boil their water.

Like all the others, Ning's face grew long and gaunt and pale. Her eyes looked like pieces of coal hiding behind her protruding cheek bones. She brought Siksik into their igloo, and one by one all the women and children piled closer, like so many listless bodies, on top of their fur-covered platform. There was comfort and warmth in being together.

One day the last scrap of food had been eaten. "We must kill our first dog tonight," Okio said quietly.

"No! No!" Ning had a wild look in her eyes. "You would kill the fattest dog, my Koko! I've been having nightmares of you doing that very thing. And I would choke to death if I were to swallow a mouthful of her meat!"

"Be sensible. We are no longer hungry, we're starving!"

While they argued, bloodcurdling screams came through their snow walls. The piercing shrieks meant only one thing. Somebody was being attacked by an animal.

Okio grabbed his gun and was outside in seconds. A starving husky was on top of Etak and in the process of tearing him to pieces. Okio plunged in and knocked the dog senseless with the butt of his gun. He pulled Etak inside, a mass of bleeding and torn flesh, and then he vanished through the snow tunnel again.

7

Koko's Narrow Escape

Itow came to life as though she were a child startled out of a deep sleep, and she was at Etak's side before anyone else could reach him. During the days of hunger her frail body had shrivelled, and her joints had stiffened. But now they became nimble, for there was a need for her old but skillful hands, and she shed her stupor as though it were a cumbersome caribou cover.

"Light our last candle for my dull eyes." She began giving orders as she stripped the boy to assess his wounds. The roll of soft caribou which she kept for just such an emergency was quickly brought out.

Etak moaned with pain and opened his dazed eyes. "I killed one of our dogs—was bringing the meat here—Siko slipped his collar—he attacked—" Then mercifully he slipped into unconsciousness.

"We can be thankful it wasn't a bear that had his claws into the boy's flesh." Itow's deft hands were wiping the wounds and then covering them with caribou-skin dressings, using pressure where it was needed. "There is healing in this soft fur," she muttered, as the last area of raw flesh was being covered.

Etak lay so still and white in his many bandages that a deathlike silence gradually stole over everyone. "Will he live?" they whispered in an undertone of anxiety.

"The poor, motherless boy will live," Itow sighed wearily. "But the tendons in his left leg and arm are so badly torn that he will never hunt with the hunters." Tears were trickling down her wrinkled, leathery cheeks as she spoke the sad words.

Okio had returned to the igloo while his grandmother was speaking, and he flinched at her words. "I had a purpose in leaving so quickly," he explained. "I shot the dog that attacked Etak, so there are now two dogs to be eaten. And here is a *pok-sac* of seal oil that Father Komoyiok left me, for such a time as this." Okio seemed to become a man as he laid the meat and the seal oil at his mother's feet.

"Now we must eat!" Atuk drew on her hidden source of courage. Never had so many lives depended on her. But she was the lady of the igloo, and as long as she had a breath in her body, every guest and family member would be looked after. She sent Okio hurrying out for a large, snow block and she encouraged the others. "There will be hot tea to put warmth in our bodies, and meat for our stomachs. After we have eaten and watched the bright glow of the seal oil lamp, sleep will come to us, and we will feel better."

They did eat, and as they watched the golden flickering of the lamp, in their hearts they thanked the Great Spirit.

Each day that followed there was meat for one meal, and hot tea from time to time. No one questioned the source of the meat, nor did they interfere as Tuliak and

Okio consulted quietly with Etak each time the supply ran low. They were the men of the settlement, and they were doing their duty.

"At least everybody is being kept alive," Ning tried to comfort her mother, as they worked together looking after the packed igloo during the day. At nighttime they slept lightly, for Etak rolled and tossed because of the nightmare that stayed with him, whether awake or asleep.

"Yes, child. But what of our men? They are out in the cold darkness and will not return until—"

"But they are the Iniut!" Ning interrupted. "They feel such pride in the land of their ancestors that they will fight the enemies as they meet them. It is true they will come back with frozen faces, but their heads will be held high, for they will be the masters. Has it not always been so?"

"Yes. Yes." Atuk took fresh courage from the child. "We are the Iniut! And this is our land."

All track of time had been lost, and no one cared, for the struggle to live had dulled their senses. There seemed to be no time other than the present, and their world became the size of the igloo that sheltered them. That is, until the day the hunters returned!

Like conquerors, the three who had gone seal hunting arrived first. Two fat seals were hauled into the igloo, but the people could do little more than stare. They were sure it was a horrid dream that had become beautiful. Nevertheless, their hands reached out.

"No part of this seal will be eaten until we have thanked the Giver." Komoyiok knelt in their midst and thanked the God of the Iniut for the nourishment that would bring life back to their cold, listless bodies.

Almost mechanically, they ate the meat. But it was scarcely any time until warm waves began tingling through their bodies, right down to their toes and into their fingertips. "Our faces are shining like the seal-oil lamp!" Ning exclaimed excitedly, as she watched the soft, warm glow reach their cheeks.

Komoyiok finally had to restrain their eating. Not only was there tomorrow to think about, but their stomachs had shrunken over the long period of hunger. But never had blubber and seal meat tasted so sweet and tender!

On the same day the bear hunters returned, but they had only some fox carcasses and one rabbit to show for their days in the moonlit wilderness.

After two more sleeps, Etak's father, Nigalik, and his companion were back. "It's not much we bring," they sighed, hanging their heads sadly, for they had only an armful of fish to add to the food supply.

"But you are all back safely!" the women and children cried out in relief. "We now have the strength to go to the lake and fish for tom-cod. We can endure it, for we know the worst is over."

The menfolk examined Etak's wounds with grave eyes. "Leave him in our igloo, " Itow begged his father. "As you can see, his wounds are healing, and I spend much time rubbing his muscles with seal oil."

Nigalik nodded approval and staggered back to his lonely igloo. For a while he sat on the snow platform shaking his head in unbelief. Death had taken his two younger children and then his wife. "And now my son is maimed!" he cried out in anguish.

While the rest of the igloo village slept in deep silence, Nigalik tossed in his grief, and sleep would come only in short snatches. Out of one of these snatches he sat up and found himself bathed in sweat. In his dreams, wild animals had been tearing at him from every direction. So real were his fears that he snatched his gun. There were noises outside the igloo that seemed like part of his dream. He rubbed his eyes to make sure he was awake. He was awake, and the noises grew louder as they became real.

With the greatest caution he made his way out under the moonlight. *"Nanuk!"* His heart was pounding like a skin drum as he aimed squarely at the bear's heart. He pulled the trigger.

"Bang! Bang!" The whole snow village leaped out of their sleep to see what strange thing had happened. Right before their eyes the huge bear gave its last struggle. It seemed too good to be true, for now their time of hunger was *really* over. Or could it be a moonlight mirage playing tricks on them?

Tuliak was the first to speak. "Our menfolk risked their very lives to go in search of such a bear as this. They would have been better to have saved their frozen bodies and stayed in the shelter of the igloo. For out of the darkness the bear decided to pay us a visit."

"Not so." Siksik spoke with his usual wisdom. "If our men had sat in their igloos there would have been no scent of bait in the air to entice the bear. Their courage has paid off, and we owe much thanks to Nigalik for giving the bear such a great welcome!"

"Yes!" the children cried out. "The welcome was so warm that Nanuk decided to stay with us!" They clapped and danced in a circle around the bear, as though it were the return of the sun instead of the dead of winter.

Then suddenly Ning streaked toward the dogline like an arrow shot from its bow. Such shrieks of joy followed that even the excitement of the bear was forgotten for the time being. "You're alive!" Her arms were around Koko's neck as she snuggled into her thick fur. "And all this time

JNHOWARD

I thought we had eaten you!" Happy tears spilled down her cheeks and froze into icicles before tinkling to the frozen snow.

By this time the crowd had moved from the bear and circled around Ning and her husky. She looked up in embarrassment, for they were laughing at her childish emotions. They reminded her that no husky was worth crying over when hunger gnawed at the stomachs of their people.

"But I did try to be brave," Ning stammered awkwardly. "One night I was sure the meat tasted like Koko's! It made me feel sick—but I still ate it."

"Indeed, you are a brave girl." Siksik took her by the hand and led her to his igloo, leaving the others to celebrate the killing of the bear. The minute they were by themselves, Ning threw her arms around the old man's neck and sobbed as though her heart would break.

"There, there, child." He stroked her shiny black hair. "A good cry is what you need. You've been helping your mother look after your baby brother and all the rest of us. All the time your heart was sore because you thought Koko was no more, but not once did you whimper or complain. It's proud I am to be your grandfather."

Finally the sobbing ended, and Ning smiled through her tears. "But it seems strange that my bravery left me the instant I laid my eyes on Koko. When I knew for sure it wasn't her ghost, I felt as weak as a newborn lemming, and I'll still be shedding tears in my sleep. Can you still be proud of me?"

"Indeed, I can." Siksik patted her hand. "There are many things I am unable to explain, so I just don't try. But my little girl brings joy to all around her, and who cares if she has a good cry when she feels like it? Now run along, and have fun with the others. But first take this—" he reached over and handed her one of the tom-cods he had jigged through the lake ice—"to Koko."

Ning grasped the fish and rubbed noses with her grand-father, then dashed out to Koko. This time she went quietly.

8

An Igloo Christmas

Ning knew that no sleep would come to her that night until she had thanked her brother for saving Koko's life. "After all, she was the fattest husky on the dog line, and to use your own words, she was useless as well." She looked at Okio with loving and grateful eyes. "As long as I live I can never forget your kindness."

"Keep your thanks," Okio answered her gruffly and a bit uncomfortably. "She would have been my first choice, except that I talked it over with Tuliak and Etak, and between us we decided that her next litter of pups would replace the dogs we had to kill. So she better have seven instead of five the next time!"

"Then I must thank somebody, for my heart is simply bursting with gratitude!" Ning turned to Etak, who was still living in their igloo. "It's no secret that Okio and I have many quarrels over Koko. You heard for yourself that my favorite dog would have been his first victim, except for the fact that she raises beautiful pups!" Ning then directed her conversation to all the menfolk. "But I feel it in my bones that Koko has the kind of meat that gives indigestion to anyone who would dare eat her. I got sick just from thinking that I was eating her meat, so you can just imagine how one would feel if it really *were* Koko. I daresay the person might die! You would all do well to remember my words if ever we come through another such hunger spell!" She sat down on the snow bench with a triumphant expression.

Okio thought he would explode with anger. Who did she think she was to give such advice to Eskimo men? He turned to his father for support and expected to hear such a blast that Ning would be silenced for the rest of the night. But Komoyiok was shaking uncontrollably, with his head bowed low. Okio knew very well that he was laughing! It was quite beyond his understanding how a mighty hunter could be so soft with such a silly girl.

When Komoyiok did speak, it was to change the subject. "It seems strange to me that we sit here talking about dogs when Christmas is so close at hand."

Christmas! They all looked mystified. They had been covered so long with a blanket of darkness that Christmas had become a dream in the far beyond.

"When do we leave?" Ning's usual excitement came to the fore when the news had sunk in. "I have only to close my eyes, and I can see a beautiful picture of golden igloos dotted over the hills around the white man's settlement. People are running back and forth to visit each other, and they go to the trade store. Every evening these same people trek to the mission. But on Christmas day they—"

"Let someone else talk," Okio interrupted irritably. He was thinking about their sorry-looking dog team. "Do you think our few huskies are fit for the long trek?" he asked Komoyiok.

"I hardly know what to think." Komoyiok rubbed his brow. "Our dogs are a skinny lot as well as few in numbers. Besides, we have very few fox pelts to trade for supplies."

"But their fur is soft and thick," Ning chimed in.

"That's right," Komoyiok agreed. "Nature is kind and has a way of looking after animals in the worst of winters. The dogs are kept warm in spite of their leanness, and the fox pelts will grade well this year."

Strange to say, it was Itow, all unknowing, who made their Christmas plans. The following morning she collapsed as she tried to get out of her sleeping bag, and she lay back in a weak stupor. Komoyiok and Atuk rolled her in soft furs, and Ning sat by her side on the snow platform for the rest of the day. The Eskimo men met for a discussion, and when it was over, their families learned the arrangements that had been made.

"We will not be going into the white man's settlement to celebrate Christmas this year," Komoyiok announced to his igloo members. Nigalik will hitch his dogs with ours to make one team, and he will trade our pelts for the supplies we must have. The others will double up and make the journey by going slowly."

"Does that mean our family will be here all alone?" Ning asked, a little stunned.

"That is right," Komoyiok nodded. "You know your grandmother will not be able to travel, and Siksik prefers to stay with us. Also, Etak—" he looked with compassion at the boy sitting at the edge of the snow bench—"will be much better here. That is, unless the disappointment will be too great?"

"I would much rather stay here," Etak said without hesitation, "for I lack the courage to have all those people staring at me with sorry eyes. I'm almost a cripple, and it's still more like a fearful dream than the truth." He hung his head as though he had brought shame to his people.

"Indeed, you have plenty of courage," Komoyiok replied in a husky voice, "and we're glad you will stay to be company for all of us. Come with me, and we will help the others get packed for the long slow trek." And he assisted Etak outside.

Ning's disappointment passed quickly, and she began counting her blessings. Her grandmother had started to rally, and she would nurse her back to health. This would be her very first Christmas to have a grandfather—and a baby brother! And were there any parents in the whole world that compared with her own? she wondered. Away down deep, she knew Okio was a good brother, even if they did quarrel a lot. It was sad to think of Etak, but he could so easily have been killed that having him was another blessing. And there was food in abundance.

"Christmas is a time of happiness," she whispered softly into her grandmother's ear, as she patted her cheek. And Ning made a vow that she would do her part in making it happy for everyone.

But try as she would, Ning could not keep the tears back when the time came to say good-bye to Mituk. They knew they would not see each other for a long, long time, and as the sleds pulled away, some part of Ning's heart seemed to tear away and go with her friend. There were so many things she could not understand, and Mituk's sadness about her marriage was a burden to her heart.

However, the dark days passed quickly, and life was bright inside the igloo, for Grandmother Itow improved rapidly and almost seemed better than before her sickness. In the evenings Siksik told stories that held them spellbound, and they played games with fine, sealskin strings on their fingers, and the igloo echoed with laughter.

"Who would exchange all our fun for the big celebrations in the settlement?" Ning asked loudly on Christmas Eve. Then she added almost mournfully, "But we will miss the Christmas services at the mission, and all the stories of Jesus—especially the Christmas story."

Itow laid her arm on Ning's shoulder. "As you know, this is my first Christmas as a believer in the one Great Spirit. I've had much time to think, especially during those long days in my sleeping bag. Since I speak my thoughts so poorly, I made up a message in folklore. Would you like to hear it, this Christmas Eve?"

"Yes! Yes!" Ning went into raptures, for she had feared her grandmother's folklore days were over.

Even Okio and Etak drew in closer so as not to miss a word of her feeble voice, and Atuk brought her baby out from the pouch in her back. She felt in her heart that this would be the last message in folklore, and she wanted the words to reach her child's ears.

The igloo was as silent as the glow of the seal-oil lamp as Itow began her Christmas message in folklore:

Let's pretend it's tonight, instead of before,
That the baby Lord Jesus, is going to be born.
We'd be here in our igloo, but hardly aware
Of the event to take place; would we even care?

Joseph would rap; he'd be shaking with fright—
"Could we come inside? just for tonight?"
Mary, behind, would crawl on her knees—
"We'd cause you no trouble, if you please."

The lady of the igloo would open the door,
And white snow she'd use to sprinkle the floor.
The grandmother would lay out many white skins;
There's nothing so good to wrap a babe in.

JNHOWARD

The children would gasp and do their part;
The dogs, they would feed with fast-beating heart.
A bright star would shine in the sky above;
The message is plain—it tells of God's love.

But Komoyiok would frown and look all about:
"This igloo's not fit; it's not even white!
I'll build a new dome of white, virgin snow,
For Mary and Joseph and the One still unknown."

The grateful guests would nod and leave with a smile;
A new, sparkling igloo had been a dream in their mind.
In the morning, all trembling, our gifts we would bring
To the baby called Jesus, that was born to be King."

"I feel just like I do at the Christmas service," Ning said, breaking the silence that followed the folklore tale. "It seems strange that you were so slow to invite Jesus into your heart, but tonight you are like a missionary to your own family."

"I have no other gift to give you, dear child. Tonight the happiness of God's love is very real to me."

"We have no need for other gifts, my good mother." Komoyiok spoke for the first time. "Your words bring God's greatest gift—not only into our igloo but into our hearts. It shames me that we can do so little in return to the One who gave us His Son."

"We can sing His songs!" Okio suggested eagerly. "Etak has a voice like a bird, and he knows the words of seven."

"We'll sing His songs," the others said in unison.

Etak led with their favorite, "Jesus Loves Me," and while their voices rose above the house of snow, bright northern lights reached down as though to link them with the heavens.

9

The Darkness Ends

"This has been my happiest Christmas!" Ning exclaimed some days later. "Never will I forget our family sitting in a circle around the seal-oil lamp and singing songs to God right from the bottom of the hearts. The igloo seemed to be fairly bursting with our joy!" She placed one arm around Siksik's neck and reminded him once again that no family was complete without a grandfather. Then she looked towards Etak with laughter in her eyes. "And we even had a guest for Christmas!"

"A guest was never more welcome," said Atuk, looking up from sewing skins. "It surprises me that you know so many songs and can speak some words from the Bible."

"Perhaps you have forgotten that I stayed in the white man's settlement the months that my mother was so sick—before she died." A lump came into his throat as he went on. "It was a time of great sadness, but the white people were very kind, and they taught me many of their words as well as some of their writing. The missionary even wanted me to go out on the big ship and continue my learning at the mission school at Aklavik."

"But you didn't want to go?" Atuk asked.

"Not really," Etak said, shaking his head, "especially when my father laughed at the idea and told the missionary I'd never become a hunter by going to school."

"I know nothing about schools," Okio admitted, "and I'd never leave the land of my ancestors to find out. It would take more courage than to fight with a bear."

"I'm glad you feel that way," laughed Ning, who never missed a chance to tease, "for a dense head was never meant for learning."

But, happy as they were, they felt the days begin to drag, and they watched the moonlit horizon for the return of their people from the settlement. "We'll have fresh supplies and hear news of the whole island!" Ning said excitedly. Then her face clouded as she mumbled in lament, "But even when they do get back, things won't be the same."

"What do you mean?" Atuk asked.

"Because of Mituk, of course." Ning was surprised that her mother had to ask. "She will be married by now, and heading across the ice to live on the mainland. She's not happy about it, and it makes me feel sad as well as lonely."

"The marriage was arranged by her father when she was a baby," Atuk sighed in resignation.

"Well, I'm glad I don't belong to her father!" Ning went over and laid her cheek against Komoyiok's strong arm. "You wouldn't send me away, would you—not ever?"

"Not ever." Komoyiok's heart was filled with words he wanted to say, but they caught in his throat.

Everyone was startled as Ning suddenly burst out giggling. "Then Eotuk and Natsook can fight it out to the bitter end—and all for nothing! But I can almost see the fierce glitter in Natsook's eyes! I'll run to you for protection!" She hugged her father.

Etak broke out into a fit of laughter. "I thought I'd never laugh again," he gasped rolling over and over on the fur-covered platform, "but her words are so funny!"

But the family was not laughing. *What outrageous tale is the child trying to tell us?* they wondered.

Komoyiok turned pale when her words sank in, and a thunderous expression came over his face. He gripped Ning by the shoulders and demanded, "Tell me the meaning of what you have just said!"

Ning spoke freely. "At Eastertime, when all our people met in the settlement, it seemed as though all the young men were looking for a wife. Eotuk spoke out very plainly and said he was waiting for me to grow older, and he'd carry me off to his tribe. Just imagine!" Ning paused a second, for she had just thought of something that had never crossed her mind before. "That would mean I would be down south with Mituk—and among the caribou! Anyway, he had barely said the words when Natsook, from the far east, got a wild look in his eyes. I thought he'd explode with rage. He said that *he* was waiting for me, and would fight to the bitter end, if necessary."

"She speaks the truth." Etak had stopped laughing when he saw the severity of Komoyiok's expression. "And I could tell you many others that have taken notice of Ningiyuk's pretty face. I daresay if they didn't fear you so much, she would have been carried off before now."

Komoyiok tightened his grip on Ning's shoulders. "This incident you speak of happened almost a year ago. Why did you not tell me about it before this?" his voice was trembling.

Ning looked vague, and then she remembered. "It happened when I could think of nothing else except the mother I had dreamed about. And I'm almost sure it was the day before my horrid accident, when my memory left me. Anyway," Ning smiled into her father's anxious eyes, "I didn't give it so much as another thought until Mituk's sorry plight touched my heart. My knees shake like a scared rabbit at the very thought of me wearing Mituk's boots."

Komoyiok wiped the sweat from his brow and gave a deep sigh. Then he did something he had not done since Ningiyuk was a toddler. He picked her up in his strong arms and threw her to the snow ceiling, not only once but five or six times.

"You treat me like a baby!" she squealed with delight.

"You are a baby!" he told her lightheartedly. "But before Easter rolls around, we are going to have a very grown-up talk."

That same night the family tribe returned, safe and sound. It was all so exciting, and before Ning had a chance to ask about Mituk, she was listening with wide eyes to tales about the land of the caribou, to which her friend had gone.

"Ah, but she is a lucky girl!" Kudloo said. "Her husband's sled was piled highest of all, with caribou carcasses and hides. See," he said, handing Ning a roll of soft skins, "she sent you this gift of fur."

Ning's eyes sparkled, and her heart felt light. With such a kind husband, it seemed that Mituk could be happy, after all. The men were talking fast and convincingly, and her hopes soared as she listened to them.

"The caribou are roaming in herds right off the mainland. We've been invited down to the land of plenty until the fat returns to our bones and our dogs are once more

JNHOWARD

sleek and strong. We would return with our sleds piled high with caribou and hides." Nigalik passed on the good news.

"But our scrawny dogs could never make that long journey," Komoyiok cautioned realistically.

"We thought of that," Kudloo said, "but they just laughed. If one fast team on a light sled would go ahead and let them know the others had started, they would come rushing to meet us with food and spare dogs. It seems that these good friends to the south of us have not forgotten the year that the caribou deserted them and they came, in desperation, to us for help. That time it was they who returned home with sleds of seal and replenished dogs."

"Well, this is certainly our lean year," Komoyiok admitted. "Let us talk more seriously about it after the sun returns."

"We certainly will!" The young men were very eager. They had never been off the island, and the thought of stalking caribou made their blood run hot.

Things settled down to the routine of winter again, but Ning found that she no longer had time to play. "I have to work so hard that even my foolish dreams have to stay in the cold, outside the igloo." She wrinkled her pug nose at the pile of fur clothing that never seemed to grow smaller. It was her job to examine each garment for tears and then to mend them well. Besides this, she scraped hides with her *ooloo* and sewed seams on new clothing until her fingers were almost raw.

Itow's eyesight had failed, and she was too weak to work any more. Atuk's face had become lined and weary since the period of hunger. "You grow thin, while the baby on your back gets as fat as a seal," Ning told her mother with some anxiety. She marveled at her mother's strength, but cold shivers ran down her spine at the thought of her mother ever being ill.

"That is life," Atuk smiled. "A poor mother I would be if it was the other way—and my heart would be heavy."

"Yes, yes," Itow agreed. "Our baby must grow fat and strong." Then she turned to Ning with urgency in her tired eyes. "You must learn to chew the soles of boots, for it seems I will soon be too useless to do that. Your mother needs all the help you can give her."

This was the one job that Ning had been dreading. Surely there must be some magic way to avoid it! But there was not. Her grandmother started the lesson by lifting a boot to her mouth and champing on the hardened sole with her strong, flattened gums. Her jaws kept clacking up and down in a firm, even rhythm, and she kept twisting the boot until every bit of the sole had been chewed. "See," she said, looking with pride at the finished work, "the sole is as soft as your skin, while before it was almost brittle from sweat and snow. Soon it would have cracked and been dangerous to wear."

Ning picked up one of her own boots and began biting the leather, here and there, with her square, white teeth. "It's put a horrid taste in my mouth!" she protested loudly.

"You should taste nothing," Itow smiled patiently. "It's because you bite so slowly. Now watch me."

"The sun is coming back!" The good news was being shouted from igloo to igloo.

"It couldn't arrive at a better time!" Ning threw the boot in the air and leaped to her feet.

"Run, child." Atuk found her fur mits. "You mustn't miss the first peak of the sun you love so well."

"But we're all coming!" Ning could not imagine anyone

missing the return of the sun. "And this will be Kiyuk's first time! And he is not going to see it from his mother's back."

Quickly she pulled him out of the pouch and dressed him in the white outfit she had made with her own fingers. It was twice his size, but she rushed outside holding the little hunter in her arms. "Do hurry!" she called back urgently to her mother and grandmother.

Tears misted her eyes as she pointed excitedly to the great, red ball that was rising in the center of the southern horizon. Each year it seemed more welcome—and more beautiful—than the year before.

10

"My Grandmother's Song"

The greeting of the sun, which was followed by a drum dance, was a happy interlude, but the bitter coldness kept on and on. It was as persistent as the wildlife was scarce.

"Our families are pale and thin," Komoyiok told the men with whom he had met to talk things over. "If we don't leave soon for the land of the caribou, neither our dogs nor our people will have the strength to travel."

"It sounds too good to be true!" Ning was happiest of all when the decision was made. Not only would she be visiting with Mituk, but on the way south they would stay for a few days at the white man's settlement. "We'll pretend it's Eastertime," Ning suggested, "and ask the missionary to tell us the Easter story. We won't have new fur outfits this year, but we'll have a fat baby to show off!"

The menfolk were apprehensive about the visit, for their pelts would never pay for the supplies they would need for the journey. "We hope the trader will permit us to owe him the pelts we expect to have in abundance at a later time," they muttered among themselves.

Grandmother Itow shook her head sadly about the

journey, for she was to be bedded down in furs and tied on top of the sled. "I'll only be added baggage and should be left behind in the igloo to freeze into my last sleep."

"No! No!" Ning rushed to her side. "That would be very wrong, for it's against the words of the Great Spirit."

"Yes, child. I know." Itow patted her hand. "But it has been the custom of our people over the years. It was never done out of wickedness, but because we were ignorant of the laws of the Great Spirit. Old people dread the thought of being a burden, and I am longing to leave for the happy hunting ground."

"You would never be a burden to us," Ning comforted her. "And you can't go to the happy hunting ground until I've finished the special song I promised for you. Remember?"

"I remember well, but I had almost given up hope," Itow smiled. "You must hurry with it, my dear child."

"It's almost ready. You'll hear it the night before we arrive at the exciting settlement. That's a promise!" They rubbed noses with affection, and then Ning hurried to help her mother pack their belongings, for they were leaving early in the morning.

"Never was I so glad to leave a camping place," Okio remarked as they pulled away from the deserted snow village.

"We agree!" a chorus went up in unison.

"But our luck is bound to change," Tuliak called cheerfully from his sled. From then on much bantering went on back and forth as they sledded over the starlit snow.

Etak was riding on his father's sled, and he, alone, remained silent. With a heavy heart he wondered what the future could hold for one who walked with a limp and

JNHOWARD

whose arm would never hold a heavy gun. He shook himself as though to shake away the memory of what had happened. It had changed his whole life. Or was it only a horrid dream?

"Who said our luck would change?" Okio grumbled, just as they were finishing their igloo for their third sleep. "We should have been in the settlement yesterday, but our dogs go so slowly that we still have a full day of hard traveling."

Neither did Atuk think their luck had changed, and her masklike face could no longer hide her anxiety.

"Our grandmother gets weaker and weaker, doesn't she?" Ning asked in a whisper, for she could sense her mother's mood.

"Yes, child. She is failing fast." Atuk clutched her daughter's hand. "I fear she will die on the journey south, if not before."

But much to everybody's delight, the old lady of their igloo seemed much better that evening. She sat up on the fur-covered platform and drank her hot soup with enjoyment. Then she insisted on amusing the baby beside her on the furs. When he tired, she took him in her arms and sang a song of the happy hunting days of his grandfather. One song after another she sang softly into his ears.

"But you mustn't tire yourself." Ning took the sleeping baby from her feeble arms. "This is the night I promised to share my folklore song. It is filled with thoughts of you, which makes it very special."

"I'm ready—and waiting." Itow eased herself into the sleeping bag and pillowed her head with furs. "Tonight is a night for songs, and thankful I am to have a granddaughter with songs in her heart!"

Ning sat with crossed legs facing the old lady. She

reached for her hand and said, "This is 'My Grandmother's Song, that I tell you.

Our people own no books with pages to open,
So folklore tales have always been spoken.
They bring to light the things of the past;
It's the truth they hold that makes them last.

But there is a book that our eyes cannot see;
It's in heaven above—one for you and for me.
The pages are filled with the deeds of our lives
And the Words that we speak, and it holds no lies.

God writes with a marker so fair and so true,
I shudder to think of many things that I do.
But if we believe that He died for our sins,
His arms are wide open to welcome us in.

When Grandmother was young, there seemed no hope;
Evil spirits took over, and loudly they spoke.
But with the Good News came such a bright light,
That the imaginary spirits took a fast flight.

This song that I sing is to give thanks above
For my grandmother's life and all of her love.
I'll never be worthy; but I'll do my best
To pass on her love when she lies at rest.

Tears I will shed. "Foolish girl," she would chide,
"As the years roll along, more wisdom you'll find.
Bright flowers will spring from moss that looks dead;
After darkness comes the sun to shine overhead."

"I am not worthy of such fine words." Tears streamed down the old grandmother's deep-seamed face, and she could say no more.

Okio looked up at his sister as though he were seeing her in a new light. When had this foolish, chattering girl become clever enough to make a folklore song like that? He felt very envious, too. There were so many things that he wanted to tell his good grandmother, but a lump in his throat kept choking back the words.

"You have spoken for all of us, Ningiyuk." Komoyiok sat for a long time in silence; then he ordered everyone to bed in the bright, sparkling igloo.

When morning came, Itow could not be roused from her sleep, but they journeyed on into the settlement with her tied securely on top of the sled. That night she stopped breathing.

Ning listened in a daze to the words of the missionary the next day at the cold, stone grave on the hilltop. It was not until the long procession of people had gone back to their igloos and she had crawled into her sleeping bag that tears would come to her eyes. Then on into the night she sobbed as though her heart would break. No one disturbed her, for they understood.

When she opened her eyes after a long sleep, her mother was sitting on the snow platform beside her. "Life must go on," Atuk said bravely, "and there are to be more changes in our tribal family. Etak will be staying in the settlement in the care of the white folks."

"Whyever will he be staying here?" Ning asked. "Is he not even coming to the mainland with us?"

Atuk shook her head. "The white people agree that he will never be able to live as one of us. They have persuaded him to stay and learn as much as he can from them until shiptime; then the missionary will arrange for him to go out to the mission school for more learning. When he returns, he will work as an interpreter for one of the three white families."

"Is he happy or sad?" Ning asked.

“I expect he is sad,” Atuk sighed, “but we think he has chosen wisely.” Then, looking at her daughter with kindly concern, she asked, “Since you cried most of the night and have lost so much sleep of late, attending to your grandmother, would you like to stay in bed and rest for the day?”

“No, no.” Ning began to get dressed. “I feel happiness for my grandmother, now. Yesterday the words of the missionary seemed far away, but now they are ringing in my ears. He made her death seem like a happy arrival instead of a sad departure. It was beautiful—like Easter.”

“Yes, child. I thought of the Easter story too. But we will feel a great loneliness, too. Work is a good thing at a time like this, and the journey across the sea ice will be no little chore.”

“Across the sea ice? When do we leave?” Ning was wide eyed.

“In the morning.” Atuk smiled. “Your father is getting the best nine dogs together, and we hope to make a fast trip.”

11

An Igloo Tea Party

Eight days later, Komoyiok and his family were approaching a brand new country. At least, it seemed that way to Ning. "It's so smooth and gentle," were her first words when land came into sight.

"It makes our rock island look as though it had been torn up by a huge giant." Okio was sizing up the difference with a sharp eye. "We don't even have a sprinkle of earth to cover up the rough edges."

"Those must be trees!" Ning was pointing to bushy objects that were visible through the snow.

"No. One must go farther south to find trees," Komoyiok told them. "Those are shrubs and willows. I suppose you could say they are trees that will never grow up. Berries grow close to the ground here, and the flowers last much longer than ours."

"I'm sure I'd like the berries—whatever they are," Ning said. But she was not going to fall in love with their flowers. "*Our* flowers are touched with magic, for they spring out of bits of moss. Besides, they brought new life to my grandmother's eyes every summer they appeared. They are special flowers."

"You speak the truth." Their thoughts went out in deep respect to the one who was no longer with them.

"But your grandmother wouldn't want sadness." Komoyiok turned their thoughts again to the new land. "You can understand why the *tuktu* (caribou) stay here, where there is plenty of grass and lichen."

They scanned the horizon, hoping for a glimpse of tuktu roaming sloping hills. Their legs were no longer tired from the endless walking. Instead, they tingled to set foot on the land of the *tuktu*.

Suddenly the weary dogs broke into a gallop, and at the same time, dozens of tiny, black specks appeared on the ice, in the distance. It was their friends—the Iniut! They were coming out to escort them into their igloo village. Mituk was in their midst.

"You look so happy!" was Ning's surprised greeting. "And all the time I've been shedding tears, because you were far away and lonely."

"And I've been shedding tears for you, up there, in that land of hunger!" They embraced and laughed with tears in their eyes.

Never did visitors receive greater hospitality, but everything was being done in such a rush that Ning felt breathless. In the morning, five teams with scarcely more than food and snow knives on the sleds were leaving to bring the others down. Tired as he was, Komoyiok was driving one of the teams so that he could guide and help the transition. He was leaving his family in a well-built igloo, where they would have plenty of food and would be looked after.

"Take special care of my grandfather," Ning called, waving to her father. She had wept because he could not come with them.

"I'll bring him back on this sled," Komoyiok promised.

And with a flourish of the whip, the teams were on their way.

Atuk and her children began making the rounds of the igloos, for this was expected of them. But Ning did not get any farther than Mituk's new home. They had so much to talk about they hardly knew where to start. "It's just as it was in your parents igloo." Ning seemed amused. "Except that now you scrape skins and sew for your mother-in-law instead of for your mother."

"There's one big difference!" Mituk's stature seemed to grow as she set Ning right. "For now I have a husband. And someday we will have sons that look exactly like him." Then she burst into giggling as she had so often in the past. "Is Nigvik not a handsome man? Did you notice how tall and strong he is? And he can run like a caribou!"

"Indeed, he is handsome," Ning had to agree. But not for anything would she say that he looked old enough to be her father!

"You'll never be sorry you made this trip." Their chatter went on and on. Finally, Mituk came out with what was really on her mind. "Eotuk has been waiting to see you, with love in his eyes. He is a good hunter and could—"

"I must find my mother," Ning interrupted. A blank look had come over her face. She did not want even Mituk making her plans—or learning her feelings. She ran swiftly from igloo to igloo until she found the security of her mother.

"I've a surprise for you." Atuk smiled at her daughter. "These kind ladies are holding a special tea party in our honor this afternoon. It's to be in the big igloo where they gather to worship God and to hold their drum dances. Every lady in the snow village will be there."

JNHOWARD

"It's one exciting thing after the other!" Ning exclaimed.

"Yes," Atuk agreed. "And your brother is roaming the hills with a gun in his hands."

"But since I'm a girl I must go to a tea party!" Ning spoke the words from habit, but, down deep, she no longer envied Okio.

The tea party was a success, right from the start. But when Ning saw all the women gathering in, a shyness came over her. She was being treated, with her mother, as a grown-up guest! They were seated on a white-robed snow bench, and the women gathered around them. The ladies shook hands and gave them a broad grin of welcome—just as though they had newly arrived. Then it seemed every woman's right to examine their fur clothing, both inside and out. *One would think we did not know how to sew!* Ning felt indignant when they turned up the bottom of her artigue to examine the stitches and fancy border.

"Ah, but it's good sewing, and a splendid pattern!" Their low mutterings turned into loud praises. That was when Ning and her mother knew they had passed the test of approval.

Then it was time for tea. Great pots of boiling water hung over the three *kudleks,* and even though there was a scum of caribou hair on the water, it was overlooked. No one minded the least bit. A handful of tea was thrown in each pot, and the usual cry, *"Teetoritsee!"* echoed in the white dome. Everyone circled the pots and dipped in their mugs. They drank the tea, hair and all, as though it were ambrosia.

Next came the food, and Ning's eyes almost popped when she saw the menu. Each lady was handed a caribou leg, neatly skinned but with the hoof still attached. "Since the meat is close to the bone, it is very sweet." They encouraged Ning when she seemed hesitant.

There was no hesitation on the part of the hostesses. They brought out their *ooloos* and skillfully sliced the meat off in long strips, and one end of the strip automatically went into their mouths. But Ning flinched at the next stage. They flourished their knives in a quick, circular swish, and cut the meat off at the point of their nose.

"Does it sometimes happen that a nose is cut off?" Ning asked the lady sitting beside her, a little fearfully.

"No," she was reassured, "that would be very bad manners."

The meat was sweet, and Ning soon felt proficient at cutting it off the bone. But she refused to wield the knife in front of her nose—for fear she would have bad manners!

After the tea and food came the social hour, and conversation flowed freely. One lady complained that the pain in her knuckles was so bad that her sewing was like that of a child. "My family is so poorly dressed that it shames me," she said mournfully.

"Indeed, your stitches look good to us," the others told her, "and your family will always be well dressed."

Another woman was worried about her worn-down teeth. "I'm such a poor wife that my husband must surely be looking for another! This time he will pick one with youth in her favor—and strong, white teeth."

They laughed her out of her depression and told her she would be strong competition, even to one with good, chewing teeth.

The young girls giggled among themselves and let it be known that they could neither sew nor chew skins. They were reassured in turns, and once again everybody was wearing a smile.

At last the party was over, and young children poured in through the snow tunnel. They cracked the bones and ate the marrow, for this was like candy to them. Then they scooped the tea leaves out of the mugs and ate them. This was a real treat, and it was all the washing the mugs would get.

"Koanna, koanna." Atuk and her daughter thanked the ladies as they got up to leave. But the party still was not complete, for the visitors were to receive gifts. They were presented with mits, boots, caribou tongues, and enough meat to last a week. They went back to their igloo with laden arms.

12

The Day of the Tuktu

The sun grew stronger, and the people danced in the evenings to the music of the skin drum. In due time Komoyiok returned with his family tribe, and the snow village was enlarged.

"How you children have grown!" Komoyiok blinked at the change he saw. "Your cheeks glow like copper, and there is fat on your bones!"

"Only one of us is a child," Ning said, pointing to her brother, "for that one has become a man. He shot a caribou the very day you left! And since that time he has been hauling home so much meat that Mother Atuk and I have been kept busy drying it. He even—"

"I shot only a few," Okio interrupted modestly, "and they are easy targets." But there was much excitement in his face, and he had things to tell his father that could not wait. "The men say that a mass migration is expected this year, and I've been hoping it wouldn't happen until you got back. I thought the small herd was quite a sight, but they tell me it is as nothing in comparison to what is to come! They come like a flood of greyish brown waves over the tundra. It's—" Okio was so choked up that no words would come.

"Lucky we are if they come this way," Komoyiok continued for him, "and it very well could be so. Usually there is an advance guard, which could be the herd you saw. Later, the main body comes through in a solid pack."

"Why do they come north?" Ning's eyes were full of wonder.

"It is to escape from a hot, inland summer, where because of the mosquitoes and the heat, many have been known to die. Instinct drives them to the sea and the islands. Let's hope they have warnings of a very hot summer!" he said, smiling.

"I wish some of them would stray all the way north to Victoria Island," Okio laughed. "They'd be cool there—and very welcome!"

"A few have been known to stray that far, but they were half-dead from exhaustion, and as skinny as a caribou could be. But we are the Iniut of fish and seal, and we don't expect caribou."

"Just as long as I have my father back, I'm not excited about the old caribou," Ning stated firmly.

"You will be, when the time comes." Okio's eyes blazed with the very thought of caribou flooding the land. "As for me, I can hardly wait for the day to come!"

The restlessness that Okio felt came over the whole camp, for small groups of caribou kept drifting their way, and each one seemed to be relaying the same message—that herds and herds were on the way!

Ning felt none of the restlessness, for she sat sewing with her mother and found much pleasure in playing with their baby when he was free to romp. In the evenings she walked over the hills with the girls, and often she brought them back to her grandfather's igloo. He entertained them with stories that held them spellbound. Some were about bears and blizzards, but mostly they told his experiences on the ice he had learned to respect so many years ago. Ning would make tea, and they would linger in his igloo until the call of *"Nekretoren!* Come for food!" reached their ears. The other girls would rush off to the igloo of the feast, but Ning would follow slowly, at Siksik's side.

One morning the dogs roused suddenly out of their sleep in the sun. One by one, they sat up with perked ears—listening. The men watched their strange actions and listened with them. They could hear nothing, so they ran to the sloping hilltop and scanned the horizon. There was nothing to see. Back to the igloos they went to keep a restless vigil. The dogs seemed to look at them with pity, and the men were sure that if the animals could but talk, they would be saying, "We know a secret, but we won't tell!"

It was not until the dogs began yipping and pulling on their restraint chains that the men went again to the hill. This time a faint, rumbling sound reached their ears. They shaded their eyes and looked. Away in the distance, brown waves were breaking over the white snow. It was the *tuktu!*

They ran back with the news and began preparing for the greatest stampede that most of them had ever seen. Women and children came pouring out of the igloos, and the huskies were in a state of frenzy.

"There will be no need for our dogs." Kakagun, the great caribou expert, began giving orders. "We must tie every one of them in such a way that they don't slip their collars. And we would be wise to have food and tea. The tuktu won't reach us for awhile, and when they come, no one will have time or thought for such things as food."

"Can't we rush down to meet them?" Okio and the boys were pacing back and forth with frustration. They could understand why the dogs were almost going wild.

"No, no." Kakagun would not hear of that. "We don't want to send them off in a westward direction. We'll wait behind the hill and do no shooting until they are directly opposite. The closer they are to the camp when we shoot them, the less distance we will have to haul the carcasses."

The drumming grew louder and louder. And by the time the hunters got into their places the click-clacking of knocking hooves filled the air.

"It is like a flood—and it comes in waves," Okio whispered in awe to his father.

"We most likely will never see the likes again." Komoyiok stared at the phenomenal sight.

Even the old-timers watched in wonder as the living mass moved slowly toward them. All of a sudden, the waves seemed to break—and turned into caribou! There were hundreds and hundreds of them! The sun blazed down, and their flashing antlers seemed to dance on their brown backs to the rhythm of their drumming feet. They became creatures of beauty.

Kakagun gave the signal. Before the sun went down there was enough meat at their feet to last into the next winter. The heavy stream of caribou seemed not to miss their fallen comrades, and the click-clacking of their hooves kept drumming on and on.

Later that night, Komoyiok and his family sat in a daze around their seal-oil lamp. The scar of hunger was still fresh on their memories—and now this!

"I'll never forget this day!" Okio kept shaking his head. "We were wise to have come to this land of plenty."

"Yes," Komoyiok agreed, "but let us remember that the trek of the caribou changes from year to year. For no known reason, they could pass many sleeps to the west next year. It's hard to believe it now, but these people have their periods of hunger just as we do."

Their conversation ended, for there was a visitor at the door. It was Eotuk. He carried a roll of new, white skins. They had been cut from the underbelly of the caribou he had shot.

"I brought you a present," he said offering them to Ning. "There is enough to make you an artigue as white as the snow."

Ning's cheeks turned red. She looked at her father. His face was expressionless. "On our island it is only the babies that wear white fur outfits. But I will accept your gift to make trousers for Kiyuk, and the rest will make beautiful trim for the borders of the family artigues. Koanna," she said shyly, as she accepted his gift.

"But I wanted you—" Eotuk did not finish the sentence, for Komoyiok's face was scowling.

"Have tea." Atuk filled a cup for the young man.

An uncomfortable silence followed, and Komoyiok soon spoke. "As soon as the meat as been well dried and the skins scraped, we will begin our journey back home."

13

Back to Rock Island

The journey back home was long and slow, for the sled runners cut into the snow, and the cutting edges of melting ice lamed the dogs. But there were birds in the sky, and seals basked beside their *aglus*. "This is our food!" they all agreed, over the first taste of blubber. And strange to say, they were longing to get back home.

"It *was* the land of plenty!" In his memory, Okio would always carry the sight of caribou flowing over the snow. "The people were so kind it was embarrassing; but it wasn't our land—or our home."

"No. It wasn't home." They shook their heads.

The white settlement was their first stop, and happy they were to pay off in caribou hides their debt to the good trader. But their stay was short, for the snow was melting fast, and they had to go by sled to the big river where they would be setting up their fish camp for the summer.

Ning ran to greet Etak. His face was long and sad. He longed to go with them for the summer fishing, and he was in a deep depression about going out to the school in the far west.

"He was happy before you arrived," the missionary told

them, "and is doing splendidly at his studies. Seeing you all has made him homesick. But the depression will pass."

Ning slipped away to be alone at her grandmother's grave on the hill. How she longed for flowers to drape over the harsh, brown stones. Tears filled her eyes, and she sank down sobbing and laid her head on one of the stones. The words of the song she had made for her grandmother came back to her, and the last verse rang as clearly in her ears as though her grandmother were speaking:

> Tears I will shed. "Foolish girl," she would chide,
> As the years roll along, more wisdom, you'll find.
> Bright flowers will spring from moss that looks dead;
> After darkness comes sunshine to shine overhead."

Ning looked up at the sun. Never had she seen it shine more brightly as it beckoned her to go on. She dried her tears and felt a new peace as she went back to her family.

When the sleds were pulling out and everybody was waving and calling loud good-bye's, Nigalik did a strange thing. He jumped back off his sled and caught his son by the arm. "I've changed my mind about leaving you," he said with a husky voice. "Come with us, and forget about the place of learning. You can do some trapping and fishing, and as long as there is a breath in my body you will not go hungry."

"*Immana!* No!" Etak surprised them all. "My courage has come back. I must go to the school, where I will learn many things." Seeing his father's sadness he tried to explain. "Our people have always believed that life can be good only if one becomes a good hunter. But there are now other ways to live a good life, even for one such as myself. I must learn—and I will find my way."

Nigalik nodded slowly and returned to his sled.

Etak waved bravely until the sleds were out of sight. His father and family tribe would not be coming to the settlement for shiptime, and it would be several years before they would meet again. Bearing the separation took all the courage he could muster.

"Much has happened since we last pitched our tents." Atuk reminded her family of Kiyuk's birth and Itow's death as well as hunger and plenty.

"It's like the white and dark design on our artigue borders," Ning said thoughtfully. "It would be of little value if there were only one color."

"Are you glad to be back home?" Atuk watched her daughter out of the corner of her eye. "Or could it be that you feel envy for your friend Mituk?"

"Of course, I'm glad to be back home! As for Mituk—" her thoughts went back to the land of the caribou—"I'm happy for her, but I feel no envy." Then bursting into giggles she added, "Her husband is *so old!*"

"You silly child!" Atuk threw restraint to the wind and hugged Ning until the girl squealed with pain.

During the summer months Ning had strange, new feelings that stirred within her. The desires to run carefree in the wind and chase the rabbits were the same as last year and the years before. Yet they brought a feeling of guilt, for back in the tent, endless skins were waiting to be scraped and sewn into clothing. Besides, there were many new things to learn—like how to dry fish. She wanted both the fun of childhood days and the accomplishments of grown-up life. Often she was brought to tears in the conflict.

But seldom a night went by that she did not go alone to watch the sunset. Once again it was dipping into the northern horizon, with the sunrise following soon after.

One night she was startled to feel her father's hand on her shoulder. "Often I follow you with my eyes, but to-night I came to disturb your daydreams by having a talk."

"That's good." Ning looked up brightly. "I still miss my grandmother, especially when the sun is setting. If she were here there are many things that I would be telling her."

"Tell me. I'm a good listener." Komoyiok sat down beside her.

"My words must sound foolish to you, but I'll tell you anyway." She looked into his steady, strong eyes. "I'm so mixed up that half of the time I don't know if I'm sad or happy. Some days I'm floating on a cloud of happiness, and the next day I might be crying, when there isn't a thing in the world to cry about." Much to her surprise she found it almost as easy to talk with her father as it had been to talk to her grandmother. She went on, "As you well know, Etualik follows me as though he were my shadow. Some-times I like his company. But mostly I don't, and we have awful quarrels. What do you think of such strange feelings as I have?"

"I think you are no longer a little girl," Komoyiok sighed. "And all the more reason why we should have a talk about your future."

"I love when you take time to talk with me." Ning hugged her knees and looked into the sunrise.

Komoyiok started right in. "You have seen the return of the sun twelve times, and many girls are married at your age. It is—"

"You came to tell me that you have chosen my hus-band!" Ning pulled away from him. Her eyes were wild with fear.

"No. No. My little girl," he caught her hand and pulled

her to himself. "I've come to say that your mother and I don't believe in child marriages. We hope you will keep thoughts of marriage out of your head and stay in our igloo for as long as you will."

"That could be forever and ever!" Ning snuggled into his shoulder as if for security.

"I doubt it." Komoyiok shook his head. "There are many who want you for a wife. I'm beginning to feel like your guardian as well as your father every time we are in a crowd."

"Guard me well against Natsook," Ning giggled, "for he frightens me."

"I'll remember your words." Komoyiok's face was grim. But he had more to say, and he looked at her with gentle eyes. "We know that we can't keep you forever and ever, as you say; for it is natural to marry. But the man that becomes your husband is to be your own choice."

Ning looked at her father with unbelieving eyes. "You said I could choose my own husband!" She repeated his words several times.

Komoyiok nodded. "You have made wise choices before."

"But am I wise enough to choose a husband?"

"That's why we want you to wait. Wisdom will come, and there can be real happiness only if you feel love for your husband."

Ning snuggled into Komoyiok's shoulder. "With such a father as you to guide me, I know I can learn to be wise." She smiled at her inner feelings. "I was all prepared to marry the man you said I must, and I would have pretended happiness. But your words make me feel free and happy. Maybe my mixed-up feelings will leave me!"

"It could be," Komoyiok said. "Words never come easy

JNHOWARD

to me, but I wanted you to know that it is no longer you who needs us as badly as we need you. Things have a strange way of changing." He rubbed his chin. "Without your fun and laughter, our home would be a hollow place. You have the strangest way of bringing the sun wherever you go—even into the igloo."

Ning thought her heart would burst with happiness. Any words that she could say would sound very foolish at a time like this. They sat watching the sun in the northern sky for a long while.

14

Ning's Choice

Three years had passed since that night Ningiyuk had sat talking with her father while the sunset embraced the dawn. She was now much taller and had blossomed into a radiant woman. Komoyiok nicknamed her Sirenek Nuligak, "my sunshine girl," and the subject of marriage was never spoken about.

Kiyuk was a four-year-old, chesty boy, and he fairly worshiped his older sister. Not much wonder, really. For baby Itow crowded him out of his mother's artigue pouch—and into Ning's arms.

Okio had grown into his father's image and could hunt almost as well. He had love in his eyes for a girl, and everyone suspected that she would soon become a family member.

Apart from the deepening seams in Atuk's face, she had remained much the same. But ever since she had accepted the Great Spirit, a new gentleness glowed in her eyes, and she was filled with love toward her family and friends.

Siksik had died a year back, and Ning had inherited a treasure of memories that would never fade.

After two years at the mission school, Etak had returned to his people. He was reconciled to the fact that he could never be a hunter, but there was contentment in his eyes, for he had found a good life. He now lived in an igloo beside the mission and reflected the teaching of Christ in his interpretations and deeds.

Etualik was still unmarried, as was Eotuk from the south and Natsook to the east. There were numerous other young men, and they all had eyes for Ningiyuk!

"They give me no peace!" Ning's face seemed to sparkle with happiness at the Easter gathering in the big settlement. Wisely, she kept close to her father. "Now they talk among themselves about a sled race. Be prepared to talk with the winner, for he will claim that he has the right to be my husband!"

"But you have not given your consent—or encouragement?" Komoyiok watched her expression closely.

"Of course not! When I choose a husband it will not be because of his fast dog team! This is talk between themselves."

"They are lining up now!" He pointed to the large crowd milling on the ice. "It looks as though the competitors are going to circle the island out in the bay and then return to the starting point."

Every team was in shipshape condition, and some even had their harnesses decorated with bright, red balls made from wool. The dogs had perked ears as though warned to be alert.

"It's a sight to behold!" Ning could not help but admire the colorful array of dogs and sleds.

But as they merged into the crowd, Komoyiok could feel strong tensions. The good-natured fun and bantering that went side by side with the spring races was miss-

JNHOWARD

ing. It was all too clear that the young men were not competing for the large, fancy can of tea that was the trader's prize. Their grim faces told him that they were racing to win a wife—his daughter.

The lineup was ready. *"Bang!"* The crack of a gun was the signal to start. The teams lunged forward like arrows released from bows. Two sleds collided. Okio's was one of them, and he pulled out of the race, for his heart was not in it.

"Eotuk leads!" the people cheered.

"Tuliak has pulled up. He is now in the lead!" They cheered and clapped louder than ever.

By this time some of the crowd had edged their way up the side of the hill in order to see better, and they called reports of the progress down to the others. But after awhile the sleds became black specks, and there was nothing else to do except to speculate about the winner. Finally the sleds had circled the island and were on the homeward stretch. One sled was far in the lead, and it came like a black streak of lightning towards them. They strained their necks and eyes to see. The winner was Natsook!

Everyone remained in silence until the rest of the teams, in turn, crossed the starting line. Then the cry went up, "Let Ningiyuk present the prize!" At the same time, someone shoved the can of tea into her hands.

She looked at her father for permission. He nodded, so she ran to Natsook with the tea. "You have a very fast team," she said as she handed him his prize.

Much to her horror, he threw the tea and grabbed her hands. "You are to be my wife! I've waited long enough!"

"No! No!" Ning screamed, and tried to free herself.

"Yes!" Natsook picked her up as though she were a feather and jumped onto his sled. With one shout to his

dogs, they galloped away, leaving the speechless crowd behind.

Komoyiok was the most speechless of them all. But in seconds he had recovered, and he leaped to Okio's empty sled. By the time he had lifted the ice anchor, Okio had thrown himself on. Together they took chase.

Atuk walked back and forth wringing her hands in their igloo. "Take care of my child!" she cried out in anguish to the Great Spirit. Then she sat down on the snow bench and pulled Kiyuk and Itow to her knees. She felt comfort in their closeness as she waited.

After what seemed like a dark winter, their team returned. Through the snow tunnel, Ning crawled on shaky knees. She was as white as the snow, and Komoyiok helped her to the snow platform. Without speaking, Atuk handed them both a mug of hot tea.

By the time Okio came in, Ning had revived. "You must give him credit for having courage!" she giggled hysterically. "I've dreamed many times that the fierce one snatched me out of my sleeping bag and galloped away. But who could even imagine that he would snatch me in front of a crowd of people? And in the presence of my own father!"

"He wouldn't do it again, little girl. I gave him the whipping he deserves!" But Komoyiok was more agitated than his wife had ever known him to be. He ordered Okio to take the children outside and leave the three of them alone.

"The time has come for you to choose a husband." He stopped his pacing and stood in front of Ning.

"Etualik came in second." Atuk spoke for the first time. Her head dropped in shame, for she had spoken out of turn.

"But the race means nothing to me!" Ning was on her feet. She pulled her parents down to the snow bench while she stood facing them. "I told you that before the race, didn't I?" She looked at her father.

"Yes," Komoyiok answered, a little gruffly. "But I think your mother is trying to tell you that Etualik is a good lad and almost like one of the family. We both like him—and approve of him."

"But you said I could choose my own husband! Haven't you noticed the love in my eyes?" her face was radiant. "I've been waiting and waiting for you to speak about it."

"Who is the *inuk* you have chosen?" Komoyiok braced his feet for the unknown answer.

"Etak is my inuk! There is much love between us, and we would marry tomorrow if you would give your permission." She looked at her father with begging eyes.

Komoyiok went limp. Etak was the last person he would have guessed. "It must be pity you feel, for he is almost a cripple. You have scarcely seen each other in three years, so how can there be feelings of love?"

"I feel no pity for Etak. He will help the missionary bring the message to our people, and because he can speak both languages, there will be a better understanding between the Iniut and the white man. And he's as brave as a bear hunter!" A mischievous glint came into Ning's eyes. "Tonight he was going to ask your permission to marry me. That takes courage from an inuk who can only fish and trap!" Then Ning stopped to think. Some things were hard to explain. "It is true that we haven't seen much of each other, but the messages that we sent back and forth when he was at the mission school made us feel close—and our love grew strong."

"Have you lost your senses, child? What messages are you talking about?"

"Oh—the messages were prayers. Do you remember that Etak almost refused to go to school? I gave him encouragement and promised to send up a prayer for him every night when the sun was setting. And on the dark days as well. It seemed to make the hard choice easier for Etak, and he said he would watch for the sunsets, too, and say a prayer for me. God not only answered our prayers, but He brought us close to each other. Does my choice not please you?" Ning's eyes were pleading for approval.

Komoyiok looked at his wife. She did not speak, but a message reached him through her eyes.

"We approve of your choice. Etak will be your inuk." Those few words meant utter happiness for Ning.

She dropped to her knees and wept on her father's knee and then on her mother's lap. "Because I'll have a husband doesn't mean that I'll love you less. I'll love you more—if possible."

"We know you will." Atuk held Ning's firm cheeks between her strong hands. She knew well that there was an unbreakable bond between them.

"And if we have a son, as I'm sure we will," Ning said, looking into her father's eyes, "he will bear your name. And you will teach your grandson to hunt."

"And if you have a daughter," Komoyiok tousled her hair," I hope she will be another sunshine girl—just like my little Ningiyuk!"

Glossary

Aglu. The breathing hole of a seal.

Artigue. The Eskimo's main fur garment, similar to a jacket with a hood.

Bannock. A bread made of oat or barley flour, baked in flat loaves.

Caribou. A type of deer with broad, flat antlers, related to the reindeer.

Char. A medium-sized fish, the Arctic salmon.

Husky. A strong, medium-sized dog with a bushy coat and curled tail, used as a sled dog by the Eskimo.

Ice floe. A flat, free mass of floating sea ice.

Inuk. Eskimo word for *man.*

Kudlek. A seal-oil stove.

Lemming. A small, tan, furry animal, similar to a guinea pig.

Lichen. A plant composed of fungus and algae which often grows on rocks.

Ooloo. A rounded knife used by Eskimo women to scrape animal skins.

Pok-sac. A pouch made of sealskin, used as a container for seal oil.

Sinew. A narrow, strong strip of animal tissue used as thread.

Soapstone. A soft stone having a soapy feel.

Snow platform. The Eskimo's living room. It is a shelf of snow a few feet higher than the floor of the igloo, covered with furs. This is where the family sits, eats, sleeps, and plays games.

Tom-cod. A small, speckled fish, similar to the codfish.